Chad waved as they started moving.

Lionel abruptly pushed his truck door shut, ran to the tow truck, and banged on Chad's door once with his open palm. The tow-truck stopped. Chad rolled down the window.

"Where are you going?" he shouted over the noise of the engine. "I was told this load had to go doubles to Indiana, and it was hot."

Chad nodded to the side of the road.

Lionel turned his head in the direction of Chad's nod.

"I've got to go with my truck," Chad said. "You're driving with Gwen."

GAIL SATTLER lives in Vancouver, BC (where you don't have to shovel rain), with her husband, three sons, dog, and countless fish, many of whom have names. She writes inspirational romance because she loves happily-ever-afters and believes God has a place in that happy ending. Visit Gail's web site at http://www.gailsattler.com.

Books by Gail Sattler

HEARTSONG PRESENTS
HP269—Walking the Dog
HP306—Piano Lessons
HP325—Gone Camping
HP358—At Arm's Length

On the Road Again

Gail Sattler

Heartsong Presents

Dedicated to Victoria. You drive like a truck driver whether you are behind the wheel of your Freightliner or your car. And that is not a bad thing.

Yer friend

A note from the author:
I love to hear from my readers! You may correspond with me by writing: **Gail Sattler**
Author Relations
PO Box 719
Uhrichsville, OH 44683

ISBN 1-57748-964-0

ON THE ROAD AGAIN

Scripture taken from the HOLY BIBLE: NEW INTERNATIONAL VERSION ®. NIV ®. Copyright © 1973, 1978, 1984 by International Bible Society. Used by permission of Zondervan Publishing House.

Cover illustration by Ron Hall.

PRINTED IN THE U.S.A.

prologue

"I hear you're going to become an auntie."

Gwen Lamont nodded. "Yes. When I teased Garrett and Robbie and said it would probably be twins, Robbie went all pale and I thought she was going to faint."

Uncle Chad snickered and sipped his coffee.

The chair next to her scraped on the floor and Garrett sat down beside her.

Gwen plunked her elbows on the table and rested her chin in her palms. "Hey, Bro'," she commented when her twin brother reappeared. "Is Robbie feeling better?"

"Yes, no thanks to you. She's lying down."

Deliberately she turned her back to her brother. "So, Uncle Chad. What's wrong? I can tell something's bothering you."

A loud sigh told her she was right. "Jeff has to take the summer off for a gallbladder operation, but I'm under contract to run doubles. I asked the boss, but he said the company can't be without the team for that long. I'm going to have to find another partner, but good drivers are hard to find."

"Oh, come on, Uncle Chad. I'm sure lots of people can drive a truck. How hard could it be?"

Garrett made a strange sound under his breath but didn't comment.

Uncle Chad slammed his fist into the table. "It's much harder to drive a truck than people think."

"Oh, come on now. The hardest part would be having to sit next to you for days on end."

"I didn't think you, of all people, would be like this, Gwen."

She couldn't hold back her laugh. "Why? I speak the truth."

She felt a poke in her arm. She turned to her brother. "What?"

"If it's so easy, prove it. You have all summer off."

"Pardon me?"

He crossed his arms over his chest and leaned back. "I dare ya."

"You've got to be kidding."

Garrett jerked his head toward their uncle. "If you think driving a semi is so easy, *you* can be the temporary driver."

"It's called a tractor-trailer, not a semi," Uncle Chad muttered under his breath. "Amateurs."

Both men stared at her, and she glared back at Garrett.

Over the years they had constantly challenged each other, much to the dismay of all who knew them. Seldom did either of them back down, but this time Garrett had gone too far. While it was true that, as a teacher, Gwen had all summer off and didn't have plans except for a few outings with her friends, the last thing she would ever have thought of doing would be spending all her time with Uncle Chad.

On the other hand, as a truck driver, her Uncle Chad visited lots of interesting places all over North America, even though he seldom stayed long at each spot. Sometimes it was just a day before he picked up his next load and kept going. Often he and his driving partner had remarkable tales to tell of the fascinating places they visited. As a child, she had been amazed at the stories her uncle told. He was also part of a network of Christian drivers who traveled together when their paths crossed.

Garrett was right. Once her classes for the school year were over, she had no plans for the summer. Now that her two best friends were married, one of them to her brother, she was starting to feel left out.

They continued to stare at her, and Garrett raised one eyebrow. "Forget it, Uncle Chad. She knows she can't do it."

She crossed her arms over her chest and glared back. "I

don't imagine it's much different than pulling the camper or boat, except it's bigger and heavier, and it's farther than the campsite."

Uncle Chad grunted.

"Coward," Garrett taunted.

Gwen glanced toward the calendar on the wall. She had two months and then school would be over, leaving her nothing to do but stare at her four walls.

Garrett turned to Uncle Chad. "It's not a job for a woman, anyway."

Gwen rose and stomped to the drawer and pulled out the phone book.

"What are you doing?"

"I'm making an appointment to get my Class-One license. By the last day of school, my name better be painted on the door of that rig."

Garrett laughed.

Uncle Chad groaned.

Gwen dialed. She could hardly wait till the first day of summer.

one

The blast of the air horn sounded just as Gwen stuffed the last pair of socks into her duffel bag.

"I can't believe you're really doing this."

She raised her eyes to see her friend, Molly, approaching her bedroom, one hand waving in the air as she walked. Molly's husband, Ken, stood silently in the hall, keeping a respectable distance from Gwen's room.

Gwen yanked the zipper shut. "I've got nothing better to do all summer, and Uncle Chad needs the help."

Molly planted her fists on her hips. "But you just barely got home from school and you're already leaving. We were planning a party to see you off. You're going to be gone before everyone's here."

Gwen hitched the strap over her shoulder, then grabbed her camera. "The load's gotta go."

Molly snorted. "You sound like a truck driver."

"I *am* a truck driver. Starting right now."

She walked past Molly, smiled a greeting at Ken, then walked through the living room. Garrett sat on the couch with their mother, eating the goodies that were supposed to be for the party. He waved, then popped another meatball into his mouth, but she caught the wink and the approving gleam in his eye before she left the room.

A few of her friends and her Aunt Chelsea surrounded the truck, which was parked in front of the house. Uncle Chad bowed from his position beside the passenger door and pointed to the scripted handwriting next to the door handle.

"You did it!" Gwen gasped. "That's my name on your truck!"

Aunt Chelsea poked her husband in the ribs. "Don't get too excited, Gwen, dear. It's not permanent. It will only last until the next rain, I'm afraid. So, enjoy it while you can."

Uncle Chad cleared his throat and checked his watch. "Let's get going, Gwen. We've got lots of miles to make by dawn Monday."

She opened the door and was in the process of hoisting herself up into the cab when Robbie's voice sounded behind her. "I can't believe you're doing this, Gwen."

Gwen laughed. "I think I'm hearing an echo. Molly just said the same thing."

"Doesn't that tell you something?"

She pushed her duffel bag and camera behind her into the bunk, closed the door, fastened her seat belt, and leaned her head out the open window. "Yes. It tells me that I've been too predictable all my life. See you in a week or two."

With another blast of the air horn, they were on their way to the terminal to pick up their first load.

❧

Lionel Bradshaw waited for the dispatcher's signal to begin fueling, glad to be outside. All the other drivers were hanging around in the dispatch office instead of the lunchroom, and the place was getting crowded. Word had it that Chad was due into the yard shortly with his temporary driver—his niece who had the summer off from school. They all could hardly wait to see the kid and have a good laugh. Frankly, Lionel pitied the poor girl, who probably had no idea what was being said about her. He couldn't help but be annoyed at Chad. He should have seen this coming and found someone else.

Sometimes drivers brought along wives or girlfriends who had their Class-One, claiming that they actually drove when their own allotment of driving time was up. But those women didn't really drive. They were a ruse so the driver could make more miles without getting caught on an infraction. Everyone knew what was really going on. Short of someone falling asleep at the wheel, there was no way to catch them. Lionel praised the Lord that such an accident hadn't happened to anyone there yet, but everyone knew, one day it would.

He could understand if, in desperation, Chad had asked a nephew to help drive, regardless of a young age, but a *girl*. . .

Of course she had to be old enough to drive to get her Class-One license. Still, Lionel thought Chad had more sense. Most of all, he had always looked up to Chad, as a Christian brother, to do the right and honest thing.

He finished checking the oil when Chad's unit pulled up behind him at the pump. First Chad hopped out of the driver's side. Then the passenger door opened.

It wasn't a girl who hopped out at all, but a gorgeous, dark-haired woman about ten years older than the student he'd been expecting—a woman who would rival many men for height. Even though she wore sneakers, she walked smoothly and evenly, with the grace of a model.

"Lionel, this is my niece Gwen. She's going to drive with me for the summer until Jeff comes back."

She stood in front of him and extended her hand. "Pleased to meet you, Lionel."

Despite her height, she had delicate hands. Woman's hands. Lionel quickly checked his palm for grease, then wiped it on his jeans, just in case. "Yeah," he muttered as he returned her handshake. "Same."

She stood almost eye-to-eye with him, probably not more than an inch shorter than he, not breaking eye contact. Her boldness was one thing in her favor, but he knew she couldn't possibly be prepared for what awaited her inside the dispatch office. Even Lionel couldn't stand the off-color remarks and had left.

Lionel finished fueling and pulled his truck forward to allow Chad to drive up to the pump. Rather than going back to the dispatch office, he remained outside to check her out without everyone else watching.

"Uncle Chad? The man in the window waved so you can get your gas now."

"It's not 'gas,' it's diesel. And we call it fuel."

"Oops."

Lionel frowned. She would never survive. Obviously, she didn't know what she was doing.

While Chad filled his tank, Lionel and Chad talked about the upcoming routine maintenance on their units. He couldn't help but notice her soaking in every word, even though she added nothing to the conversation.

When they were done, they walked into the dispatch office together to get their running orders. The room fell into silence, and Burt, the dispatcher, raised his eyes from the calculator. "Lionel, your load'll be ready soon. You've got a set of dry joints for Casper." He turned to Chad. "So this is your new driver. I'm Burt. You have a high cube van for Bismarck. The rear's dragging and the yard shunt is hooking the switch, so you've gotta slide the bogeys." He stared straight at Gwen, waiting for a response.

Her face went blank and, without moving her head, she quickly glanced at Chad, who nodded ever so slightly.

She smiled at Burt. "No problem," she said.

A number of muffled snickers echoed in the room. Lionel didn't laugh. In a way, he felt sorry for her. Burt had deliberately tried to intimidate her. When he'd first started driving, it had taken him a while to understand the lingo. As a new driver he had been allowed a lot of leeway, but he could see they wouldn't cut any slack for Chad's niece. Simply because she was a woman, she would face a certain amount of ridicule with their own company drivers, but he wondered if she had any idea what she was in for once she got out on the road, where it was survival of the fittest.

Now that the show was over, rather than file into the lunchroom with everyone else, he joined Chad and Gwen as they went outside and prepared to leave.

She glanced back and forth between the two men. "I have no idea what he just said. They didn't talk like that in driving school."

"Burt's just trying to confuse you with the lingo. Don't worry about it."

"Lingo? That was another language."

"He just meant that John's busy hooking up Dave's load and we have to adjust the axle weights ourselves if we want to get going sooner." Chad turned to him. "Lionel, you want to help slide the bogeys?"

"Sure."

Chad headed for his truck while Lionel led Gwen to a trailer in the rear of the complex.

"Why do I have a feeling that the bogeys we're talking about have nothing to do with Humphrey Bogart?"

He couldn't help but smile. He was glad she wasn't going to let Burt bother her. He said nothing.

"I'm really a teacher, you know. But if I'm going to do this for the summer, I want to do it right."

"We're going to adjust the axle weights by sliding the trailer wheels."

They waited while Chad backed up his rig to hook up to the trailer.

"Now that he's under, we have to crank up the dolly legs."

He was about to grab the dolly handle, but Gwen beat him to it and began cranking. "I'll do it. It's not much different from our camper."

He had to give her credit. It wasn't easy, but unlike any other woman he had seen, she was actually working instead of watching.

Once the landing supports were fastened up under the trailer, he led Gwen to the rear and pointed to the track. "The back axle slides along the frame rails. You set the back brakes, pull the pins, and, in this case, Chad will pull the trailer forward while the bogeys," he patted the back tire, "stay in place, which puts the wheels closer to the back of the trailer to shift the weight distribution. Each hole shifts the weight about three hundred pounds. Then we put the pins back in, release the brakes, and send it over the scale. And hopefully we got it right and won't have to do it again."

She ducked her head underneath and looked at the frame rails. "So that's sliding the bogeys."

Lionel nodded. Chad stuck his head out of the window. Lionel pulled out the pins, waved his hand in a forward motion, and held four fingers in the air with the other hand. "Ahead four holes!" he yelled.

"This is called a long box," Gwen said.

He nodded.

"It's fifty-three feet long."

He nodded again.

"It's got a reefer, but we won't know until we get the paperwork if we have to keep it running, right?"

Lionel shook his head. They were such elementary comments, but it meant she was trying to understand. "This is also an insulated trailer, but this one is equipped with what we call a heater, only meant to keep a load from freezing in the winter. Since it's summer you don't have to worry about stuff freezing."

"Oh."

The trailer groaned, heaved, then finally slid smoothly ahead four holes. Chad hopped out of the truck. Lionel replaced the pins, locked them, and Chad checked everything. "Gwen, you take the set over the scale, and I'll go get the paperwork."

"Uh, okay."

There was no need for him to stay there, so Lionel accompanied Chad to the office while Gwen climbed into the cab.

They had not gone far when the engine roared, a big puff of black smoke poured out, the truck lurched, then went silent.

The engine chugged to a start again, and this time it moved forward toward the scale, slowly, if not quite smoothly.

"Are you sure you're doing the right thing with someone right out of driving school? And have you heard what the guys have been saying about you getting your niece to drive?"

"She may be inexperienced, but I have a lot of faith in her. Gwen is my niece and she's capable of whatever she puts her mind to. We all made our mistakes when we started."

While Chad went into the office, Lionel waited outside, watching Gwen scale the load more slowly than anyone he had ever seen. He clenched his jaw. Yes, he'd made mistakes, but he had the support of all the other drivers. All Gwen would have was Chad.

"Hey, Lionel. You're ready to go now, too. Coming with me?"

He watched her pull the load onto the street and park it. She didn't know the difference between gas and diesel, but the woman had at least managed to scale the load without running into the shed. "Yeah. I think I will."

ॐ

Once they were out of the city, Gwen picked up the handset for the CB radio and reached down to turn it on while Uncle Chad drove. "What's our handle?"

"CJ. For Chad and Jeff. But you can think of your own. Lionel's handle is Lion King."

"I wasn't thinking of calling him in particular. But I guess he's better than no one."

Uncle Chad laughed. "I'm sure Lionel would be pleased to hear that."

Gwen giggled, grateful for the chance to relieve some stress. She'd anticipated a few snide remarks, but she hadn't expected to be laughed at. No one knew she'd heard, but she'd picked up on a few of the things being said about her behind her back, especially after she stalled the truck on the way to the scale. She knew she would have to work extra hard to earn any degree of respect in this predominantly male profession. Still, she thought the drivers where Uncle Chad worked would have behaved better, if for no other reason than company loyalty to one of their own.

Apparently not.

At least Lionel had helped her, although he was not exactly enthusiastic.

"Lionel is a Christian, you know."

"It must be nice to have someone you can relate to on the road. Some of the drivers are pretty rough around the edges, aren't they?"

"Yes, they are. And Lionel's single, too. And your age. And he's not bad-looking, I mean, as far as young men go."

Gwen squeezed her eyes shut. She couldn't deny anything her uncle said about Lionel, especially the good-looking part. He wore his dark blond hair in a lazy, barely-combed-back style, looking like it would fall into his eyes at any moment, yet it never did. His hairstyle served to bring attention to the dark green of his eyes, which were particularly mesmerizing. His eyes added to the mystique of his lovely smile, a feature he didn't appear to display very often. His nose had a small bump, indicating it had been broken at one time. The combination gave him an almost standoffish appearance, which probably suited the solitary life of a trucker.

"Don't start on me, Uncle Chad. I know Garrett and Robbie and now Molly and Ken are happily married, but I am perfectly satisfied with my life the way it is. I'm not on the lookout for a husband. If God places my Mr. Right in my path, fine. If not, that's fine, too."

"He's a good Christian man. Well grounded in his faith, and he lives a Godly life."

Gwen sighed and bent to check out the buttons and dials on the main unit of the CB radio. "He's a truck driver."

"I've been a truck driver all my life. It's an honest living, and there's nothing wrong with that."

She rested the handset in her lap. "For you, no. But I couldn't live like that. You're away so often for such long stretches, and then, when Aunt Chelsea is used to you being gone all the time, all of a sudden you're home again, sometimes without leaving the house for days. You're either totally absent or underfoot. That would drive me nuts. I don't know how you two do it."

"You're right, Gwen. It's not an easy lifestyle."

"And I know how hard it was for Jenny and Sarah. So many times you weren't there for their school concerts or their youth group functions. I know you tried your best to be around for the really important stuff, but I know many times they were disappointed when you couldn't be there."

She couldn't help but see the sadness in her uncle's eyes. "I know," he said quietly. "Being a truck driver is all I've ever done, and I'll do it until I retire. Your Aunt Chelsea is a remarkable woman. The divorce rate is very high among truck drivers. God has really held us together throughout the course of our marriage. But, thanks to laptop computers and E-mail, staying in touch with family and friends has been easier over the last few years. Most of the truck stops have E-mail access these days. And, with cell phones, if either of us gets lonely or an emergency happens, instead of having to track us down wherever we are in the continent and leave a message we won't get for hours or even days, now we're just a phone call away. It's sure better than it used to be."

"I'm sorry, Uncle Chad. I need more of a regular lifestyle than that. I could never marry a truck driver."

"You don't have to marry Lionel to be nice to him."

"I was nice to him. I just don't want to start anything. Okay?"

"Okay. Now go ahead and call him. I know you're dying to play with that CB."

She grinned as she turned on the main switch. The radio crackled for a couple of seconds while she adjusted the channel. "I don't know what to call myself. Mind if I just use your handle?"

"Oh, sure."

"CJ calling Lion King. You got your ears on, good buddy? Do you copy? Over."

"Lion King. Over."

"Uh, Gwen," Uncle Chad said softly before she could think of something worthwhile to say to Lionel. "Truck drivers don't always talk like that on the CB. Especially if it's just the two of us on at the moment. Just talk normal."

Gwen gritted her teeth. Something else she had done wrong. "Oops." She pressed the button to talk to Lionel. "I just wanted to test the CB. How far is the range on this thing? Over."

"About five miles. Over."

"Really? That's not a lot. And I don't know what to say. Is it true that you talk back and forth on this thing for hours and hours while you're driving?"

She waited, but there was only silence.

"Gwen," Uncle Chad mumbled, "you're supposed to say 'over.' "

"Oops." She pushed the button again. "Over."

She heard him laughing over the radio. "It took me a while to get used to that, but now it's second nature."

Gwen exchanged smiles with Uncle Chad but remained silent since he hadn't said "over."

Lionel's voice again came over the radio. "And yes, truckers really do talk on these things for hours. It helps fight the boredom through some of the long stretches, and sometimes, when we've been driving too long in the middle of the night, the chatter helps keep us awake. You can ask Chad about that some time. Over."

She continued to chat with Lionel, every once in a while giving the handset to her uncle. When all topics were exhausted, they turned the radio off.

"The laptop is behind me under the bunk. How would you like to type up an E-mail to your Aunt Chelsea, or maybe Garrett? We're going to stop in about half an hour and have dinner, and the truck stop has E-mail access."

"Really? You mean I can type while we're driving?"

"If the battery is low, I've got a converter to plug it into the cigarette lighter."

"Gee. I had no idea driving a truck was so much fun!"

Uncle Chad smiled thinly but didn't comment.

She typed a couple of short E-mails but had difficulty concentrating. Her mind kept drifting back to Lionel. Chatting with him back and forth on the CB was comfortable. Just like talking on the phone with an old friend she hadn't seen for years. Although, she suspected she would be saying the word *over,* in her dreams tonight. She couldn't remember much of what they said, but he had a wonderful sense of humor. At the same time, she sensed a closely guarded heart, which was no surprise. The lifestyle of a truck driver was very much the life of a loner, and he was a trucker by choice.

Being a teacher, Gwen was usually in the middle of a crowd of people, either in her high school classroom all day long or in adult church activities on evenings and weekends. She loved being busy. Even though she couldn't relate to someone who chose to stay solitary most of the time, she could respect his choice. Uncle Chad had been a trucker all his life, and he fit into both ends of the social spectrum. He was active in his church and with his family, when he was in town.

By the time they arrived at the truck stop, she had managed to compose two E-mail messages. She sent them off and they joined Lionel in the restaurant. Gwen had never been so hungry in her life, although she could not figure out why, since they'd been sitting most of the time. She chalked it up to the excitement of her first truck driving job and, after they paused for a word of thanks over their supper, she ate gustily.

"I've never seen a woman eat like you."

Gwen paused mid-chew to see Lionel watching her. She gulped down her mouthful and dabbed her mouth with her napkin. "I'm really lucky, I've never had to watch my weight. Guess it's because I'm so tall and have a high metabolism."

Uncle Chad nodded. "This is nothing. You should see her twin brother."

Lionel's eyebrows raised.

"Uncle Chad!"

"Never mind. We don't have time to sit and drink coffee. We've got to make Bismarck by Monday morning and, because this is your first trip, we'll be making more stops than usual. Make a quick visit into the washroom. This is the last time we're stopping for a long time."

Gwen tossed the money for her portion of the meal on the table and stood. She had been warned. This was the life of a trucker, and she had committed herself to nearly two months of this. "I'll be right back."

Uncle Chad was waiting for her in the truck.

"You've got to pay close attention to the way you shift in the mountains," he said. "We'll be arriving in St. Regis at about three A.M. I'll explain as we go."

"You mean we're driving through the mountains at night? We're not stopping somewhere to sleep?"

"In tourist season we want to avoid driving in the mountains during the daytime."

"You didn't tell me that before."

"I didn't? I'm sure I did. People tend to drive crazy around trucks. Even if we're driving faster, they still feel they have to pass us. Campers are especially bad, because often people aren't used to pulling the weight, and they don't leave themselves enough time to pass. I've been in countless close calls. So the best solution is to drive as much as possible at night during tourist season."

There were so many things he'd told her in the past about the business of truck driving, but Gwen was positive this hadn't been one of them. If so, she might have changed her mind.

"Is Lionel going to be with us, too?"

"Yup."

"And are you two going to yap on the CB?"

"Nope. Need both hands. There's a lot of shifting. You watch and learn. Didn't they take you through the mountains in driving school?"

"They did. We went up to Squamish, and I learned how to use the Jake brake, but that's nothing like going through these mountains."

"Nope. Got a few tricky corners, and in the daytime, lots of traffic."

Gwen cringed. She sat in silence as he drove, listening to her uncle explain why he shifted and changed speeds when he did. Every once in a while she glanced behind them in the rearview mirror to see Lionel's rig following behind.

❧

"We're making good time. But I'm almost out of hours. We're going to stop in St. Regis and sleep."

Gwen looked behind her at the bunks. She had been inside Uncle Chad's truck before, but it was another matter to live in it for two months with only the occasional stop at home. She wondered who got the top bunk and what she would do about the bathroom in the morning.

"For your first trip, Lionel and I will sleep in the trucks, and you can stay in motels. You need a good night's sleep, because you're driving in the morning."

two

The waitress refilled their coffee mugs and dropped a handful of cream portions onto the table. Lionel added two of them to his coffee and talked to Gwen as he stirred. "You ready for this?"

She nodded and sipped her coffee without saying a word, which somehow didn't surprise him. After they parked their rigs at the truck stop following her first trip through the mountains at night, he noted that, although she was tired, she wasn't rattled. The three of them had enjoyed a pleasant chat as he and Chad walked her to the motel. He had teased her about getting a good night's sleep before her first long driving day. Instead of being nervous, she told him how much she anticipated driving the next morning.

And now it was the next morning and they were almost ready to go.

She took another sip of her coffee, leaving the cup at her lips as she spoke. "So now we get *fuel*," she enunciated slowly, glancing back and forth between himself and Chad with a teasing twinkle in her eyes. "Just exactly how much *fuel* does a truck hold?"

Chad had just taken a large bite of his cinnamon bun, so Lionel answered. "Two hundred and twenty gallons. We get *fuel*," he drawled out, "once a day."

"See. I'm learning. By the end of the summer everyone will think I'm a seasoned driver."

Lionel chose to reserve judgment. Just because she knew the difference between gas and diesel, that didn't make her an experienced driver, or even a good one. So far, the only actual driving he'd seen was when she pulled over the scale, and she'd stalled the engine. Today he planned to see for himself what she was like on the road.

"Uncle Chad said that we wouldn't usually stop so often, but for my first trip they've allowed us extra time, the same as a single driver. I feel bad to be slowing things down."

Lionel smiled and continued to talk as Chad ate in silence. "They always make allowances for a first trip. Just one word of advice: Keep careful records in your logbook. Government regulations are very strict. When you're trying to make miles, every quarter hour counts. Don't count fueling or even when you have to take a. . .uh, stop to visit the ladies room or pick up a snack as driving time. If you take a quarter hour off driving time, log it as such. The minutes add up. When you're out of driving hours, that's it. You have to stop. And a lot of companies do random checks to compare your tach card with your log entry, not only to make sure you weren't speeding, but to compare when you were stopped with what your logbook says."

"Thanks for the advice." She stopped to grin, and all Lionel could do was stare. He didn't have much experience with women, especially considering the lifestyle of a long-haul trucker, but Gwen was not what he expected. Gwen wore simple and comfortably worn clothes. Her dark shoulder-length hair was combed neatly, but she hadn't fussed with it. Nor did she wear any makeup. If she had tried to flirt or act provocative, it would have had an opposite effect. Her relaxed nature impressed him more than anything.

He didn't meet many of the drivers' wives. They tended to stay in the trucks, hiding from the surly drivers. Sometimes, though, some of the drivers brought girlfriends who openly tried to impress their men. Often they tried to impress any man in sight, and they dressed accordingly. Of course, the truck stop "lizards" always caked on their makeup and they all wore provocative clothing to lure the men. The entire package sickened him. He had spent many hours praying for those women, unable to understand why anyone would want to live a life so full of sin. Both before and after he made his career choice as a truck driver, he'd seen this tragedy repeated often. He hadn't been raised in a Christian home, but he had been taught right from wrong. Since becoming a Christian in his early twenties, his heart had always gone out to women who would throw themselves away like that.

Unlike any other woman he'd known, Gwen didn't act like she cared if she impressed anyone. She obviously didn't care if she impressed him. And by now Lionel was certain that Chad had told Gwen he was single. That fact didn't seem to make a difference, and he was relieved.

On their walk back, after seeing Gwen to her motel room last night, Chad had made a point of telling him Gwen was single, too. Lionel had replied that, quite honestly, he had no interest in a relationship, including and especially one with his niece.

&

Chad checked his watch. "We should have been moving half an hour ago. Let's get going."

They made a quick check of the pins, trailer seals, brakes, and the air lines, and were soon ready to go. Gwen hoisted herself up into the driver's seat, and Chad climbed slowly into the passenger side, stretched, and settled in, as if he didn't have a care in the world. It wasn't the way Lionel would have felt if a beginner were driving his truck.

Slowly the truck inched to the highway entrance. At least this time she didn't stall the engine.

The truck entered the highway, jerking and speeding up a little more each time she shifted until finally reaching the posted highway speed limit. Soon he was driving behind them, which was where he wanted to be in case they had trouble.

He didn't hear from them on the CB all morning, although he didn't think it was because she was too scared to operate the radio while driving. Instead, he suspected Chad was explaining things as they were going.

The first time he heard from them was lunchtime, and that was only long enough to learn that they were pulling off at the next rest area for a sandwich. Lionel always anticipated the first lunch stop on a new trip if he was traveling with Chad. Chad's wife stocked his fridge with all sorts of yummy treats, and Chad always shared. Eating at too many greasy-spoon restaurants over the years had given him an appreciation for a nice cold sandwich and fresh fruit.

When he pulled in, Gwen and Chad already had a few bags containing their lunch piled on one of the picnic tables.

"Aunt Chelsea sure makes a great lunch. And now I remember where I learned to pack the fridge in the camper in a way that makes use of every single square inch of space. Who wants grapes?"

He noticed she didn't wait for a reply before placing a sandwich and a small handful of grapes on each of three plates. Then she left the rest in a bag in the center of the table.

Lionel stared down at their lunches. "Paper plates? We're eating on paper plates?"

"Oops, I forgot the napkins."

"Napkins?"

When Gwen ran back to the truck, Chad turned and whispered to him, "The wife included them this time, just for Gwen."

Gwen hustled back and handed out napkins, along with pieces of cake, each on a fresh paper plate, a plastic fork tucked neatly on the side. "This is just like camping, except I wash dishes instead of using disposable stuff. It's more environmentally friendly."

Lionel picked up one of the utensils in question. "Plastic forks, too?" He shook his head. "Gwen, we travel as light as possible, and that doesn't include tableware. We eat fast, so the sandwich doesn't get put down, and the same with the cake. Then we just go."

"If you eat too fast, you'll get indigestion."

"I've never had indigestion, and I've been doing this for ten years."

"Well, you're just lucky."

"Luck's got nothing to do with it. I'm perfectly capable of eating sensibly, and I do, most of the time."

"Do you know the four basic food groups?"

He crossed his arms over his chest. "Bread, dairy, meat, and fruit and vegetables. Do you brush your teeth after every meal?"

She stuck up her chin at him, scrunched up her nose, and bared her teeth at him.

Lionel barely suppressed his laugh. She could give it right back to him, and he liked that. "Okay. But do you floss?" he asked. "And do you—"

Chad raised one hand, cutting him off before he could finish his sentence. "Stop bickering and let's eat."

After a short prayer of thanks, they ate.

Most of the women he knew picked and nibbled at their food, but when Gwen ate, she ate every bit as fast as he did, and she ate just as much. Yesterday, when they stopped for supper, he couldn't help but notice how much she'd eaten. Now he was wondering if this wasn't unusual for her.

Their hands bumped as they both reached for the last grape in the bag.

He grinned. "Who gets the last one?"

The second he hesitated, she grabbed it and popped it into her mouth. "Me. If you snooze, you lose. I put everything out, so you clean up. I'm making a trip to the little girls' room."

Before he could protest, she was gone.

Chad snickered beside him. "Did I tell you that her brother usually doesn't have a chance?"

Lionel looked down at the empty bag. "Thanks for the warning."

Again Lionel followed them down the highway, but this time they chatted on the CB. For a while they discussed an interesting topic her pastor had brought up at the last church service. He was surprised and pleased when she offered to get him a tape of that particular sermon and leave it in his mail slot at the home terminal when she got back. It wasn't as often as he would have liked that he could attend a service, for he spent most weekends on the road. Whenever he could, he tried to be at one of the truck stops which scheduled informal, non-denominational services.

They drove straight through to Billings, arriving at the rest area on the edge of town as the sun was setting. Chad had made coffee before they arrived for a last quick break together, for, from here, they would be going separate ways.

Gwen hopped out of the driver's side, reached her arms to the sky, and twisted her back. She froze and blushed when she caught him watching. "I guess I'm not used to sitting for so long. I've never thought about what it would be like."

Lionel smiled. "You get used to it. The seats are built well, with good back support; some have special custom adjustments. Still, it helps to get out and walk around whenever you can to try and stay in shape."

She pressed her fists into the small of her back and arched. "Yeah, I can see that. And that sounds like a good idea. Who wants to go for a walk?"

Chad shook his head as he settled in with his coffee. "Not me. I like being fat and out of shape."

Lionel looked around the nearly deserted park. He didn't think it was a good idea for a woman to be walking alone in a place like this at nightfall, but he suspected she would go anyway. "I could probably use a stretch. I'll go with you."

They helped themselves to the coffee and began their walk with mugs in hand.

"So how was your first day driving?"

"Good. My last couple of shifts I never missed a gear. But truck driving is a lot different than what I expected."

Lionel figured as much. If she thought she was going on a

joy ride, she'd probably had a rude awakening. Most of the girlfriends and wives who came along only wanted to see the countryside. Since she was a teacher with the summer off, he suspected Gwen was expecting to experience a cross-continental summer vacation and get paid for it as a bonus. "Most women find that," he said.

"I knew a lot of people drove like idiots around the trucks, but I had no idea it was this bad. They have no concept of just how big or how heavy that truck is, and because of that, how long it takes to stop, and that we can't make split-second maneuvers. They just think we can simply turn the wheel and zip out of the way for them when they do something stupid."

Her response caught him off guard. He had been expecting her to say something about not being able to stop and check out the scenery. "Summer is the worst season for bad drivers."

"Uncle Chad said the same thing. Tourists. Some guy, with his wife beside him and a car full of kids in the back seat, just whipped in front of me and cut me off when it took him longer to pass than he thought. Then he got mad when I was too close to his bumper until I could slow down. You should have seen him, I could tell he was swearing at me. And then the kids poked their heads in the back window and stuck their tongues out at me."

He sipped his coffee. "Unfortunately, that kind of thing happens all the time."

She turned to him and smiled. Even in the twilight, she had a lovely smile. His heartbeat picked up speed and his throat tightened.

"Yeah. Uncle Chad calls them four-wheelers. That's so funny."

He cleared his throat. "Yeah. Real funny."

He listened to her expound on her driving experiences of the day, but rather than hearing what she said, he paid more attention to how she said it. Instead of carrying on like a kid with a new toy, albeit a rather big toy, she was making comments he could relate to as a fellow driver. Her thoughts and impressions were the same as his own on his first few trips.

Chad's voice echoed from the distance. "Come on, you two! Time to get moving!"

Gwen giggled, and it was a lovely, happy sound. "Oops. Sorry. I didn't mean to yak your ear off."

They hustled back to the trucks, and he noted that this time Chad was driving. They entered the highway, and at the intersection he replied to the blast of their air horn with a short blast from his and turned right while Chad and Gwen continued.

He wanted to turn on the CB, but didn't since in only a few minutes they would be out of range. The silence disturbed him more than it ever had before. For the first time in ten years, Lionel felt lonely.

He turned on the radio louder than usual and headed for Casper.

ↄ⋒

Gwen ran her finger down the map. "We're almost there. He said he'd be at Salt Lake City about ten, so we're right on time."

Uncle Chad applied the Jake brake to slow the engine. "Yes, but it was strange of Lionel to send an E-mail. I can't remember the last time I got one from him."

"Really? I thought you would be in contact with him a lot."

"No. Remember, we didn't become truck drivers because of our typing skills."

Gwen could not hold back her laughter. The last few days were an education like she had never imagined. After they'd delivered their first load, even though she knew they wouldn't be dispatched straight back to home, she'd expected to at least head in that direction. Instead, they'd been sent to some place in Iowa, and then to Denver. Finally they were heading in the right direction, even if they wouldn't be back to Vancouver and her nice soft bed for another three or four days.

More than her bed, what she most looked forward to was her bathtub.

The truck stops had functional showers where the drivers could see to their personal needs and then move on, without necessarily sleeping. She compared it to a library, where a person would borrow a book, relax for a short while, and then leave. Renting a shower seemed a bit strange. However, since the drivers basically lived in their trucks, there was definitely a need for such amenities.

While most of the truckers she met were generally friendly, many had trouble with the idea of a woman on a driving team and not merely being along for the ride. She also found a great many of them lacking in social skills. Her uncle tried to take their stopovers in the Christian-oriented truck stops when they could, but when traveling in a straight line to make time, they didn't have any choice when they had to stop at a place that wasn't so nice.

For this trip, when they stopped for the night, she slept in the motels or rented a room at the truck stop and Uncle Chad slept in the truck. Next trip, they would be taking turns, one sleeping while the other drove, like a real doubles team.

"He beat us. There's his truck."

Gwen raised her head. Although the highway was dark, the parking lot of the truck stop was well lit. Like any typical summer evening in Salt Lake City, the outside temperature was still more than comfortably warm. Instead of waiting for them inside the coffee shop, Lionel was sitting on his running board, his legs stretched out, his head leaning back against the part of the cab that stuck out where the sleeper began. He looked like he was sleeping, but she knew he couldn't be. She'd been learning, the hard way, to rest in strange places and positions.

"Gwen, honey, I'm not feeling great. I think I need a little sleep. You go in with Lionel and I'll grab some Zs in here."

"Are you okay? You're not coming down with something, are you?"

He shook his head. "Probably not. Your Aunt Chelsea packed me a new bottle of vitamin C, so I'll take a few and lie down. Now go stretch your legs."

She didn't want to leave him alone but had to trust that he'd been doing this all his life and knew what he was doing. She hopped out of the truck and approached Lionel, who opened his eyes and stood when she neared his truck.

"Hi," she said.

Lionel stood and brushed some dirt off his jeans. "Hi, yourself. How's the driving today?"

They started walking toward the building. "Really good. It's so amazing, the number of miles we've done in such a short time."

He held the door to the coffee shop open for her and they walked to a small table in the center of the restaurant. The waitress poured their coffees, described the specials of the day, and left them with menus.

Gwen studied the menu. It hadn't been that long since she had eaten supper, but she was already hungry. While she decided whether she should have just a muffin or go all out and have a hamburger and fries, she tried to ignore the loud group of men at the next table. Normally, she wouldn't have paid attention, and she hadn't meant to eavesdrop, but a few of the men were being so obnoxious she couldn't help but overhear. When one of them commented on his wife at home and, in the next sentence, mentioned his girlfriend in another town, Gwen's blood went cold.

"I know. It bugs me, too."

She looked up at Lionel. His mouth was drawn into a tight line, and he was holding his menu far tighter than necessary.

"As you can guess, Uncle Chad and I spent a lot of time talking about stuff like that. I know it's not an easy lifestyle, but they've both remained faithful for over thirty years."

"Most men are. It's guys like that joker at the next table who make me sick."

Gwen glanced up at Lionel. She saw more than righteous anger in his eyes. She saw pain. Infidelity, the breaking of the ultimate trust in another human being, always angered Gwen. Fortunately, she had never been involved in a relationship where she had been personally hurt by unfaithfulness. From Lionel's bleak expression, she wondered if he had. She wished she knew him well enough to talk about it.

"Hey, buddy!" A man with a tattoo of a snake on his forearm rested his elbow on the table next to them and leaned closer to their table. "Wanna introduce me to the little lady?"

Gwen stiffened.

Lionel didn't move as he muttered out of the corner of his mouth, "Get lost."

"Maybe she's not a lady."

His grip on the menu tightened even more. "She's more of a lady than you've ever met."

The man leaned back in his chair and tilted his head to comment to the rest of his friends at the table. "Hey, guys. He doesn't want to share."

Gwen couldn't believe what she was hearing. The worst part was that they were talking about her. She didn't know what to do, so she remained silent.

Lionel slapped his menu to the table. "She's a driver, not someone who would get involved with slime like you."

The man called out a crude comment and the rest of the men with him laughed uproariously. Lionel's face hardened even more and he started to open his mouth, but Gwen feared what might come out and, worse, that, once he said something, a fight would start. To prevent Lionel from speaking, she quickly laid her hand on his wrist and gave it a gentle squeeze. "Ignore them," she whispered between her teeth. "Let's just go."

His eyes narrowed and his lips tightened.

"I mean it. I wasn't hungry anyway. Let's go."

He slapped enough money on the table to cover the cost of

the two cups of coffee and they both stood.

A wolf whistle pierced her ears. The man made a very crude comment about her figure as she walked away.

Lionel's pace hesitated in front of her, but Gwen stopped dead in her tracks. Anything Lionel said at this point would instigate a fight, but as a woman she could get away with telling the man she didn't appreciate his comments. She whirled around, stomped to their table, and smacked her palm down onto the table.

"Say that to my face. But before you do, know that I am a Christian. I live my life the way God wants me to, and I'm happy. Because of God's love and what His Son, Jesus Christ, did for me, I know where I am going when my days on earth are over. Do you? Think about it. Do you have the strength to do anything other than show off to these guys from the safety of a crowd? Well, let me tell you something, *tough guy*," she sneered and leaned closer to his face. "When you're not shooting off your big mouth in front of these other *tough guys*, think of your wife, who you've cast aside like garbage. Do you think she'll stand beside you and support you when you're old and weak? Will these guys be with you then? Will anyone? I know Jesus is with me, every minute of every day. He's always there. I'll be praying for you."

Gwen stood, still fuming, her breath coming out in shallow bursts, her fists clenched tightly at her sides. Gradually she became aware that every person at every table was staring at her. Complete silence filled the room. Even the waitress stood stock still in the corner, the coffeepot in her hand.

Lionel grabbed Gwen by the hand. "We're leaving."

Without protest, she let him lead her outside to his truck. He unlocked the door, they both hopped inside, and he locked it again. "I'd offer you a coffee, but I don't think you need the caffeine." Without asking first, he reached into the fridge and handed her a juice box. "I know the place is a mess. It'll only take a minute to straighten up, though."

He kicked aside some clutter from the floor, flicked a switch to release the bunk bed, raised it, and secured it to the back wall. Next he lifted up a fold-down table and clicked it into place. The music from a popular Christian CD began to play.

"Sit down. Take a deep breath. Relax."

Gwen sank into the chair, thunked her elbows to the table, and buried her face in her hands. "I don't know what came over me."

Lionel poked the straw into the juice box and pushed it across the table toward her. "He was a pig."

She shook her head. "That's still no excuse for my behavior. That wasn't kind or loving, and that wasn't going to open his heart to Jesus."

"I don't know if kindness would be effective in a situation like that. Your delivery certainly caught the respect of everyone in the place."

Gwen raised her head.

"Seriously. I don't think anything could make him change right now. But one day your words will come back to him, and one day they might make a difference."

"Really?"

He nodded. "Oh, yes. You made an impression. And not only with the jerks at that one table."

Gwen buried her head in her hands again. She hadn't wanted to make an impression, but she couldn't deny that she had. She would never be able to show her face in that particular place again. Still, she was driving for only two months. This was Lionel's life, and after making such a scene in his company, she had just made it impossible for him to go back.

"It's difficult to be a witness for Christ on the road, but it can happen. I'm an example of that. Don't be too hard on yourself. God uses all kind of situations for His glory, even if we don't know it at the time."

Her ears perked up. Gwen had been raised in a Christian home and had made her decision to follow Christ when she was twelve. She loved to hear stories and the testimonies of people who turned their lives over to Christ when they were adults. One of the best moments of her own life was when her friend Molly became a Christian after many years of witnessing and praying for her. She had personal proof that prayer worked.

Even though she didn't know the man's name, and even though he had insulted her terribly, Gwen knew, right then, that she had to pray for him.

Lionel looked at her from across the small table. One corner of his mouth tilted up, and he reached across the table and covered both her hands with his larger ones. "Yes, let's pray for him."

She didn't know how he knew what she was thinking, but she couldn't have agreed more. They joined hands over the table and prayed for the man, for God's mercy and kindness to touch him, for the man to open his heart to salvation in Christ Jesus, and that he could become a witness to the unsaved once he turned his life around. They also prayed for the man's wife, for God to hold her up, that she could forgive her husband and their marriage could be saved.

"Amen," they said in unison.

Gwen lifted her head and opened her eyes slowly. She wasn't sure, but she thought Lionel's eyes were a little too shiny.

He blinked and turned away, causing her to wonder if the dim lights and shadows were playing tricks on her.

Lionel checked his wristwatch. "It's getting close to midnight. Chad will want to drive a few more hours before you two stop for the night, and I've got to make some miles, too. Maybe I'll catch you on the flip-flop."

Gwen stood but didn't leave the cab. Something special had passed between them. She wasn't sure what had happened, but something had. She prayed with other people all the time, but this was different.

She watched him as he prepared to make a pot of coffee. Lionel was a nice Christian man. But, even though she could see so many good things about him, she knew she could never get involved with him. All her life she had seen the heartache and disappointments her cousins endured when their father wasn't around. And her Aunt Chelsea. There were times when a woman simply needed her husband, but her uncle hadn't been there. Aunt Chelsea had never said anything specific, but Gwen could tell when her aunt was unhappy.

Gwen knew her own personality and needs well enough to know she needed more solidity and more togetherness than that from a friend, and she needed *much* more than that from the man who would be her husband.

As much as she loved her Uncle Chad, Gwen had vowed she would never get involved with a truck driver. When the summer was over and her time as a trucker was over, she would never see Lionel again. The thought saddened her, but that was life.

Yet, for now, for the summer, they could be special friends whenever they met up with each other.

Gwen opened the cab door and hopped to the ground. "I'll go wake up Uncle Chad. See you next time our paths cross."

three

Burt handed Gwen the envelope containing the running orders. "No appointment on this one. You've got to get it there as fast as you can without breaking any laws. It's a specialty piece of machinery for a plant breakdown in Evansville, Indiana. Every day they're shut down costs them ten grand, and four hundred people are out of work until you get there."

Gwen cringed. She knew the doubles teams got all the priority and rush loads, but she never thought of a situation like this.

"If you get there in the middle of the night, it doesn't matter. Call that number on the envelope when you're an hour out of town; they'll have a crew standing by, ready and waiting."

Uncle Chad nodded. "I'll drive first through the mountains, then you take over when I'm out of hours."

Gwen nodded.

They drove to the manufacturer's plant to pick up the load. When it was ready, they hooked up, made sure it was blocked properly, checked the trailer for the usual things, and, within half an hour, they were on the highway.

"This is it, Gwen. Our first real doubles trip, and it's a dandy."

"Yes." It was a tremendous responsibility, unlike any she had ever faced. Every day she accepted the accountability of her students, the mentoring and guiding of young lives, but that was on an ongoing basis. She had never before been forced into such an urgently critical situation. Now, from a different perspective, she saw Uncle Chad's job in a whole new light. Being a truck driver was more important than driving widgets from A to B. At times, people's livelihoods depended on them. Their driving skills might very possibly be the determining factor in the failure or success of a business. And, if that business happened to be a predominant industry in a small town, the fate of an entire community might rest in their hands.

This time Gwen didn't feel like chatting on the CB as the miles went by. Even though they were days away from their destination, the urgency of the need for speed was always on her mind. Unlike her first trip, when she thought they were traveling so fast, this time, considering the urgency of their load, they seemed to be moving in slow motion.

They reached the start of their journey through the mountains as darkness fell. The start of the ups and downs and the curved roads only seemed to taunt her, reminding her this would be the slowest portion of the trip.

As they continued, she watched Uncle Chad downshift, preparing to make the most difficult ascent in this section of the mountains. At least the worst part of the trip was nearly over.

"Uncle Chad? What's that noise?"

They were both silent as a ticking sound suddenly increased in volume.

"I don't like the sound of that," he muttered.

A loud bang and the grinding of metal on metal jolted the entire unit. The truck rocked and lurched as the engine seized. Gwen grabbed the door handle with one hand and braced herself against the dashboard for support while her uncle fought with the wheel, forcing the truck to the side of the road. They came to a very sudden, complete stop.

Gwen's heart pounded as she forced herself to breathe. "This is bad, isn't it?"

"I don't even have to look, I know what's happened. The truck's thrown a rod. It's very bad."

"Can you fix it?"

Through the glow of the dashboard lights, she could see a

very humorless smile on his face. "Fix it? No. I have to call a tow truck. The repairs are a major job, and very expensive. The truck will be down at least a week."

She stared into the rearview mirror at the trailer they were pulling. "What about that machinery? It's got to get to Evansville as soon as possible."

He reached between the seats and pulled out his cell phone. "They'll have to dispatch another truck to come and get it. We're not going anywhere."

❧

Lionel pulled into the terminal compound and backed his load against the fence.

The trip had been a long one, and he was tired. He'd had to wait a few hours for his load to be ready, and he'd left Portland later than usual. It was now nearly midnight. He smiled as he thought of going home and crawling into his nice soft bed for a good long sleep, since he wasn't going to be dispatched tonight.

"Here's the paperwork, Burt. See you tomorrow."

"Whoa! Lionel! Not so fast."

He waited while Burt finished a phone call and hung up.

"Sorry about this, buddy. I don't have any drivers in town with any hours left. I've got to send you out."

"Out? I've only got three hours left before I have to book off. Send me in the morning."

Burt shook his head. "No can do. Chad's broken down in Snoqualmie Pass with that hot load for Evansville. It will take you three hours to bobtail there. Then you can sleep. You're taking the doubles load. We can't delay eight hours. Get going."

Lionel fueled his truck and left as soon as he could. In nearly ten years he'd never done a doubles run, and he wasn't looking forward to it now. He didn't want to think of driving a very rush load almost all the way to the East Coast. He had just come into town after being away for over a week. All he could think of was having something to eat and going to sleep. The only good part of this trip would be that, since Chad had been dispatched from home tonight, he would have a fridge full of good food. All those goodies would be transferred to his now-barren fridge.

Thinking of Chad's fridge full of food made him think of Chad's wife. At times, Lionel was almost jealous of Chad and the closeness of his family, how they managed to overcome the trials of long absences. He used to think about coming home to a wife and kids anxious for his return, but he now knew that was a fantasy. His parents hadn't been able to keep their marriage together, no matter how much or how little time they spent together. Experience had shown him that, when put to the test, the one woman he would have called "special" turned out to be no different than his mother. Chad had indeed been blessed to have a woman like Chelsea beside him as his life's partner.

Briefly he wondered what life would be like with a special woman to welcome him home with open arms after a long absence. The first woman who came to his mind was Chad's niece. He knew Gwen was single because Chad had told him so. And, because she had chosen to take the summer and drive around the continent with Chad, Lionel had to assume that, for now, she had no one to call special. No one worth staying in town for the summer to be with. He didn't know why a woman like Gwen was still single at thirty years of age. He was thirty-one, but he knew why he was single, and he planned to stay that way.

Lionel shook his head to break away from his mental meanderings. Gwen was a teacher—a people person. She was in her element in a crowd, both with children and adults. Everyone liked her. He had seen that firsthand. Every time she came into contact with people, they warmed up to her. For someone to whom people gravitated, the temptation was too great. Absence did not make the heart grow fonder. He'd learned that the hard way.

He slowed his speed as he approached the glow of headlights near the summit of Snoqualmie. A tow truck was already hooked up to Chad's Kenworth. Lionel parked behind the rig and stood to the side. He watched as the truck was pulled out from under the trailer. Shaking slightly, the trailer settled onto the landing legs and, when it was on solid ground, the tow truck pulled Chad's truck clear.

Chad appeared at his side. "Threw a rod," he mumbled, shaking his head.

Lionel also shook his head. "Bad stuff. Down time?"

"Figure a week and a half. Maybe two."

"Taking it home?"

"Yeah. Most of the repairs should still be covered under warranty."

"Expensive towing bill."

"Figure so."

Lionel said a short prayer of thanks for Chad that, since this was a major job, the truck had broken down fairly close to home.

He turned to climb back into his own truck and get ready to hook up to the trailer, but he stopped dead in his tracks when he saw Chad climb into the passenger side of the tow truck. Chad waved as they started moving.

Lionel abruptly pushed his truck door shut, ran to the tow truck, and banged on Chad's door once with his open palm. The tow truck stopped. Chad rolled down the window.

"Where are you going?" he shouted over the noise of the engine. "I was told this load had to go doubles to Indiana and it was hot."

Chad nodded to the side of the road.

Lionel turned his head in the direction of Chad's nod.

"I've got to go with my truck," Chad said. "You're driving with Gwen."

Lionel's breath caught as he saw Gwen standing stiffly at

the side of the road beside the trailer. Her duffel bag was slung over her shoulder. A number of grocery bags and a few other items lay at her feet. Her shoulders were hunched, her arms were crossed over her chest.

This was not the same Gwen who had pitched in on her first trip to help slide the bogeys, or held her own when Burt tried to make her look foolish in front of the other drivers. She hadn't shown any sign of weakness then. The size and weight of driving a tractor-trailer unit hadn't intimidated her either. When she lost her temper at the truck stop a few days ago, her righteous indignation had instantly earned the respect of many truckers, and his, too.

Gwen now looked terrified. And all she had to do was get into his Freightliner.

"I can't drive with your niece."

"You don't have a choice. She's the other half of the doubles team, and this half of the team has to stay with the downed truck."

"I can't."

Chad sighed. "I don't like it either, but Gwen doesn't know anything about mechanics, and with this kind of job I can't leave her in charge of such an investment. Jeff just got out of the hospital; I can't expect him to look after this. Face it, the company doesn't see her as a woman. They only see a licensed driver and a load that's got to move."

"It's not that she's a woman," Lionel stammered, "it's that she's. . .female. I mean. . ." He couldn't finish the sentence. Even though she was a beginner, she was a qualified driver. He also knew she was no shrinking violet if trouble came up. So far they got along well enough when they were together, both in the serious stuff as well as the good-natured teasing. They had shared a very special moment when they'd prayed together.

What he didn't want to think about was their being together, all day and all night, without a break for over a week.

Most important, it was neither right nor proper, even if they were on the road and on the job, to travel with a woman, day and night.

His gut twisted. Being with her all day didn't bother him half so much as being with her all night.

"There're no options here, Lionel. I have to go with my truck, and Gwen is going with you. The load's already been delayed three hours. You've got to get moving."

Moving. He thought of what it would be like. Technically, in any twenty-four-hour period, on a critical load like this, both of them would drive ten hours apiece. Interspersed in those twenty hours they'd have a number of breaks totaling four hours to fuel, eat, and see to personal needs. Basically, the truck didn't stop. There would never be a time that they would be resting or sleeping at the same time. This was work.

He stiffened his back and squeezed his eyes shut. *Dear Lord, please give me strength. I can do all things through Him who strengthens me*, he prayed. It could be done, and it would be done

Lionel walked to Gwen. "I'm out of hours. I'll hook up, and then you're driving."

❧

Gwen knew she would be driving through the mountains at night at some point, but she never imagined this.

She had barely managed to get familiar with Uncle Chad's truck, and now she had to get to know this one. Most of all, she had to get used to Lionel.

He hadn't said anything, but Gwen knew Lionel wasn't comfortable with the situation. For that matter, neither was she. With Lionel in the passenger seat, she'd never felt so scrutinized in her life, including the time she took her driver's test for her Class-One license. The multiple shifts required for mountain driving were bad enough, but the job was made much worse when Lionel watched her every move. She wished the breakdown could have happened on the prairies.

Then again, if it had happened any farther from home, she wouldn't have been driving with Lionel but a stranger.

Rather than feeling sorry for herself, Gwen chose to thank God that she was teamed with someone she knew, at least a little. Most of all, even though Lionel was a man, he was Christian. And Lionel knew her uncle and, therefore, would be answering to him.

The situation could have been worse. Much worse.

She tensed with another shift, and she could see Lionel cringe, anticipating that she would grind the gears. She had done much better with Uncle Chad because Uncle Chad hadn't been worrying about his precious truck, at least not that she'd seen.

"This is your first time driving through the mountains at night, isn't it?"

Gwen stiffened. It was her first time driving a truck through the mountains, period, day or night. "Yes."

"You're doing good. I mean, for a beginner. You handled that last uphill curve really well."

"Thanks."

"Was it you or Chad driving till Snoqualmie? I'm asking because I want to know how many hours you've got left."

"I can do ten hours."

Even though the only light inside the cab was from the dash lights, she could see him sag into the seat. "Great. I've just come back from a long trip, and I was right at the end of ten hours by the time I reached Snoqualmie. I've got to have a sleep. Are you okay with that?"

"Sure."

"Wake me if you need anything. I won't be far away."

She couldn't tell if he was being sarcastic or trying to be funny. As nerve-wracking as it was to be driving alone, having him sleep instead of watching every mistake she made was infinitely better. She would rather die than wake him. "Sure."

"Stop whenever you need to have a stretch or a snack. I

probably won't wake up."

"Okay."

"If you want, I can make a pot of coffee for you before I bed down. Got any questions?"

"No questions."

Silence hung in the air. Gwen downshifted as they slowed for another hill.

"Are you always this talkative? Are you concentrating that much on your driving, or is it me?"

Gwen released a rush of air. She hadn't meant to let him know she was so tense. "I think it's a little of both."

"I guess we should talk."

What she really wanted was some silence so she could think. A million thoughts had churned through her mind while she waited the three hours for him to arrive. Now that they were actually on the way to Indiana, everything she thought she'd worked out in her mind dissolved into mush. "I suppose."

"If we're going to be living together, we should lay down some guidelines."

Gwen gripped the steering wheel so tightly her knuckles turned white. "We're not living together!"

He had the nerve to laugh. "I knew that would get you. Seriously, though, we should talk now. I don't want you to sit and stew for hours while I toss and turn trying to get some sleep. Let's get it over with so we can both relax."

She was glad for the distraction of driving. "That's a good idea."

Once more silence hung in the air. He ran his palm over his face, then pushed his hair back over his forehead. "Honestly, Gwen, I had no idea this was going to happen. The thought never occurred to me that I wouldn't be driving with Chad. I'm sorry."

His blunt honesty impressed her. "If you had known, would it have made a difference? Would you have refused the load?"

"No. I couldn't have refused, because that's ground for dismissal unless it's justifiable as a safety violation. I just wish I would have been better prepared."

"I know what you mean. I thought about it for three hours, and I'm still not prepared."

Lionel chuckled softly. "What I was thinking about more than anything else for the last three hours was Chad's fridge full of food." When she didn't join in laughing at his little joke, he cleared his throat and the humor left his voice. "Anyway, since we're stuck with each other, we should come to a few decisions and make a few agreements, although I don't know where to begin."

Gwen winced at his word *stuck*. It stung, even though she'd been thinking the same thing not long ago.

Before she allowed herself to wallow in self-pity, she recalled the routine she had developed with her uncle, and then, imagining Lionel's reaction, she couldn't stop a grin. "Who gets the bathroom first in the morning?"

"Bathroom? But. . ." His voice trailed. "Very funny."

Thankfully, the darkness hid the blush she knew flooded her cheeks. "Seriously, I've never had to think about stuff like that in quite this way, and I probably never will again. My first trip was different. We actually stopped to sleep. Uncle Chad stayed in the truck and I got a room. This isn't going to be like that, is it?"

"No. The truck won't stop except for fuel and for us to eat and stuff."

Gwen knew it might be difficult to get used to at first, but Uncle Chad was family. She could have handled that. Living out of the truck with Lionel, she didn't know. "We'll have to take things as they come, a few hours at a time, I guess."

Lionel nodded. "Yes."

"I guess you should sleep then. Is this curtain the same as the one in Uncle Chad's truck? I looked at it but never got to test it."

"They are the same, and they're very soundproof. Looks like I get to test it first. Good night, Gwen."

"Good night, Lionel."

He turned and crawled into the bunk behind the seats. The rasp of the Velcro signified the closing of the heavy Naugahyde curtain, which was double thick and insulated, covering the back area from floor to ceiling, making it as effective as a solid wall between them. Then she heard nothing except for the sounds of the engine and the hum of the tires on the pavement.

This was it. For the first time, she was truly driving alone. There was no one in the passenger seat to coach her, no one to help her when she didn't know what to do. She had known from the time she made her decision to do this for the summer that this time would come, but now that it had, everything was different.

She was on her own, in more ways than one. While technically she could ask Lionel anything, she couldn't allow him to think she was stupid beyond her inexperience.

Gwen forced herself to concentrate on her driving. In the daylight, on the flat lands, she would think about Lionel and this whole situation.

four

Gwen's stomach grumbled about the time the sun began to rise. Technically, it was breakfast time. But she had been driving all night. She was starving.

All night long she hadn't heard anything from Lionel. She'd managed to convince herself he'd be awake by the time she was ready to stop. She didn't want to embarrass either one of them, in case he slept like her brother Garrett, with his mouth open and snoring. Unfortunately, he was still sleeping, and she didn't want to find out the hard way.

The night's darkness and quiet provided the perfect opportunity for some serious thinking. As she drove down the nearly deserted highway, she tried to imagine what it would be like to be with Lionel for however long it took to deliver this load and make their way back home.

Thinking of her brother solved her problem. Gwen had always had a special relationship with Garrett, beyond that of normal siblings, because of their special bond as twins. They had been almost inseparable all their lives, and she'd missed him terribly when he moved away from home to live on-site as a park ranger and then, later, when he married Robbie. She chose to handle spending time in close quarters with Lionel the same way she did with Garrett; only this time, instead of being a brother by birth, she could relate to Lionel as a brother in Christ.

Uncle Chad spoke highly of Lionel. In fact, there were times he hadn't let up and she told him she didn't want to hear any more praises of Lionel. Gwen was tired of the attempts at matchmaking, not only from Uncle Chad, but from all her friends and family. The matchmaking intensified when she was the last one left unmarried and became even worse when she turned thirty.

Even though she didn't know Lionel well, he seemed nice enough. Still, she wasn't interested in a relationship, especially with a truck driver. The circumstance she now found herself in, and the fact that she didn't like it, proved how much she thrived on her regular school hours. She needed a more predictable and stable environment than the uncertain agenda of driving a truck. Molly and Robbie had been right. She shouldn't be doing this, but it was too late to turn back. She was obligated to Uncle Chad by her promise and bound to the company by a contract. When the summer was over, she would have learned a valuable lesson, namely, never to do something this impulsive again.

A sign up ahead indicated a place to stop, so she did. When the process of slowing down and parking still hadn't wakened Lionel, she rationalized that he must have been exhausted, so she left him to sleep and went into the restaurant without him.

"Table for one?"

Gwen cringed. "Yes." She'd never gone into a restaurant alone before.

When the waitress left her with a coffee and a menu, it felt odd not to be chatting with someone while making her selection. The awkwardness was worse after she gave the waitress her order. She would rather have prepared her own meal, in a rush or not, instead of sitting all alone in a room full of people, all of whom had someone to talk with, except for her. However, Lionel was sleeping beside the fridge, preventing her access, so she had no other choice if she wanted to eat. Next time she planned to make a sandwich before he went to sleep.

Instead of letting the time drag until her meal arrived, Gwen pulled her latest Heartsong Presents out of her purse and read until the waitress returned. She continued to read as she ate, trying to ignore the stares of people as they passed on the way to their own tables. As much as she enjoyed the book, she vowed never to eat alone in a restaurant again. She paid the bill without lingering and hurried back to the truck.

She finally heard the rasp of the Velcro curtain opening as she started the engine. Lionel poked his head through the opening. He winced and blinked with the morning light, then stepped into the center of the cab wearing a well-used T-shirt and wrinkled jeans. This time the lock of hair that forever threatened to fall into his face really had. And then some.

"Good morning," she said. "Have a good sleep?"

He grunted something she didn't understand and left the truck carrying a small duffel bag. She couldn't tell if he was annoyed with her for some reason she couldn't fathom, or if he simply wasn't a morning person. Gwen killed the engine, pulled her book out of her purse, and settled into the passenger seat so she wouldn't have to think about it.

She re-read the same page three times before she slapped the book shut in frustration. With the curtain open, she couldn't shake the overwhelming sensation that she didn't belong here, that she was invading Lionel's personal space, and that she was an unwelcome visitor in his home. With his belongings and blanket and pillow strewn around the bunk behind her, which she tried to ignore, it only emphasized that this truck was his home and she was trespassing.

At the sound of the door opening, she opened the book as if she had been reading the entire time he was gone. Lionel hopped up into the cab freshly shaven, wearing new clothes, his hair combed and slightly damp, and unlike on his departure, he was smiling.

He nodded at her as she remained sitting. "Sorry, but you're in my chair. You have to keep driving. I haven't booked off for eight hours yet." He held up a small paper bag. "I gather you've already eaten, so I bought myself a muffin for breakfast, and I fully intend to eat it now 'cause it's still warm. Want me to make coffee, and we can get moving?"

"Sure."

All traces of his earlier mood were gone, making her think that, perhaps, she had imagined it. Since he wasn't talking, she shuffled into the driver's seat and tried, once more, to read until the coffee was made and it was okay to start driving. Despite the lack of conversation, he still distracted her, and she still didn't finish that page.

Gwen studied him out of the corner of her eye as she pretended to read. She couldn't detect any signs of discomfort or nervousness. Unlike her, he seemed relaxed and perfectly content making coffee for the two of them before they carried on with their day. While the coffee dripped, he tidied up. He organized his personal effects, raised and secured the bunk, and stowed a few things in the overhead storage bins.

The atmosphere felt entirely too domestic, and she didn't like it.

He squatted to open the small fridge. "You take your coffee with milk and one sugar, right?"

"Uh, yes, I do," she mumbled, refusing to be pleased that he remembered.

He poured two cups of coffee into travel mugs and tucked them into slots in the dash. "Ready. Away we go."

Gwen tucked the book into her purse, pushed her purse behind her and under the bunk, buckled her seat belt, and turned the key. He said nothing as she inched to the highway entrance, and he remained silent as she went through the process of shifting and accelerating until she was up to highway speed.

Once they were traveling smoothly, he lifted his coffee out of the holder and sipped it slowly. "I wasn't sure how well I'd sleep in a moving truck, but I was out like a light. I briefly remember a bit of a disturbance, which must have been when you pulled into the truck stop, but I must have gone right back to sleep."

Gwen checked her watch. "You didn't get that much sleep. It's only been six hours."

"That's as much as, if not more than, most truckers get in

one stretch on the road. It's more like a series of long naps than bedding down for the night."

Now she was convinced she wasn't cut out for this life. She hadn't discussed the nitty-gritty of sleeping schedules with Uncle Chad, but she needed a good night's sleep, every night, on an ongoing basis.

"Are you getting tired, Gwen? It's probably been a long day for you. If you want to stop, we can."

"I'm okay. Besides, it's only another couple of hours and we can trade spots."

She remained silent while Lionel bit into his muffin.

The silence didn't last long. "So, is driving a truck all you thought it would be?"

She laughed a very humorless laugh. "It's nothing like what I thought it would be."

"It's kind of a skewed home-away-from-home kind of thing. I spend more time in my truck than I do in my apartment."

"You probably don't have a single live plant, do you?"

"Yes, I do. I have a cactus. It's not doing too good, though."

Gwen didn't comment.

He took another bite of his muffin, closing his eyes while he savored it. "This is sure different than trying to grab a bite while I'm driving. I could get used to this."

"Don't count on it," Gwen mumbled.

"Did you say something?"

Gwen shook her head. "Nothing worth repeating."

Silence hung in the air while he held the mug close to his face, inhaled the heady scent of the coffee, and then drew a long sip. As he spoke, his deep voice made a strange echo inside the metal cup. "I've never done team driving before. I've often wondered what it would be like, day after day with the same person. I would think they would have to be very unique friends."

"I guess. Or relatives."

He tucked the mug back into the holder. "That doesn't

count. I know Chad is your uncle, but that was only a temporary arrangement. I'm thinking about Chad and Jeff. They've
been a driving team for, must be, twenty years. They spend
more time with each other than they do with their wives."

"That's true." She'd thought about that very thing over and
over and still didn't have an answer as to how or why it
worked. The inside of the truck seemed a lot like her family's
camper. Every bit of space was well planned, every square
inch used. But it was still not very big when two people spent
days, or even weeks, at a time in it without a chance to get
away from each other.

He nodded and popped the last of the muffin into his
mouth. "I've been asked to run doubles a few times, but I like
things just the way they are. I'll always run single."

From what she'd seen, Gwen didn't doubt that. Lionel very
much fit the image of a loner. She worried that, because of
this fact, there would be an uncomfortable silence between
them. However, that had not been the case so far. To the other
extreme, for a supposed loner, he talked an awful lot. "I've
noticed that your truck is different inside than Uncle Chad's."

Gwen listened while he explained the differences in design.
Apparently Uncle Chad's truck was one of the few makes that
came from the factory with the standard option of bunk beds,
which gave Uncle Chad and Jeff more space to call their own
in a very limited environment. Needing only one bed, Lionel
had chosen the option of a fold-down table.

If a person didn't get claustrophobic, Gwen could see how a
person could live like this, because the cab wasn't too much different from a motor home interior, except smaller and without
cooking facilities. The only bad part: There was no bathroom.

Lionel checked his watch. "Well, that's an eight-hour break
for me. And minus the stop back there, that's about seven
hours of driving time for you, which is plenty for a beginner.
Want to trade places, as soon as we find a place to pull off?"

Just the thought of taking a break made Gwen sag. It hurt

her pride for him to suggest she needed preferential treatment as a beginner, but the truth was that she was tired of driving. "Yes, I'd like that."

She drove in silence while Lionel told her more about the different options and what life was like living out of a truck, until they reached the next rest area.

Rather than switching places and continuing, they hopped outside for some fresh air. Lionel jerked one thumb over his shoulder in the direction of the picnic area. "Let's have a short walk, and then away we go."

Gwen eyed the ladies room. "In a minute."

&

Lionel flipped on the cruise control once they reached highway speed. He hadn't expected to sleep well, but to his surprise, he had. Unlike every other rush trip, where he had to grab a quick bite on the run, or eat while he drove, he'd enjoyed his breakfast at a leisurely pace. More than that, he'd enjoyed having someone to talk with in a private, quiet, and smoke-free setting.

He'd suggested to Gwen that, rather than crawling straight into the bunk, she ride for a while and wind down. Even though she was exhausted from her first long stint of driving alone, she took his advice and was now sitting beside him staring out the side window in silence.

"I see you brought a sleeping bag and your own pillow."

She nodded but didn't turn her head. "Yes. I was supposed to get the top bunk, and I didn't want to use Jeff's personal stuff."

He'd noticed exactly what she brought, since he had helped carry everything from the side of the road into his cab. Besides the sleeping bag and pillow, she had exactly one duffel bag, her purse, and a camera. He didn't know a woman could travel without half a dozen suitcases. He'd carried more bags of food from Chad's fridge than Gwen's personal effects.

"I guess by now Chad is back home and everyone knows what happened. Do you want to E-mail your family and tell them everything is okay?" At least he *hoped* everything was okay. She'd been so quiet he didn't know what she was thinking, and he didn't know why it mattered to him what she thought. Gwen was just another driver, and this was just another job, and very soon it would all be over. Life would be back to normal and he would be alone in his truck once again.

She turned her head. "That's a great idea! I'd forgotten you could do that."

"The laptop is in the lower compartment, on the same side as the fridge."

He didn't want to interrupt, nor did he want to intrude. She focused all her attention on the computer while she typed, then turned it off.

"I'm going to sleep now. Is it okay if I tuck this under the seat? I'll sleep better knowing you won't have to crawl under the bunk to pull it back out again."

Lionel sighed. "I guess this is one of those things that we knew would come up when we talked yesterday." He waited for her to respond, but she didn't. "We're probably going to have some awkward moments since we're going to be in close quarters for a long time. I want to be sure we respect each other's privacy and personal space. If you ever want some time alone when we're moving, just go to the back and close the curtain, and don't worry about hurting my feelings or anything like that. I don't want to invade your privacy, and that includes going underneath the bunk if you're on top of it, sleeping or not. And I trust you'd have the same courtesy for me. If that curtain is closed, it stays closed unless there's an emergency."

He glanced quickly at her, then returned his attention to the road.

"That sounds good. I think I'm going to go to sleep now. The bunk is easy to take down, isn't it?"

"Yes, it works on a hydraulic mechanism. Just undo the clips; they're easy to figure out. See how it's done?"

"Yes, I can figure it out. Thanks."

The bunk thumped slightly as it settled into place. The curtain slid closed, and the rasp of the Velcro announced the finality of the separation.

He had wanted to say good night or something but couldn't figure out exactly what to say. Now he'd missed his chance.

Lionel reached for the CD player, but his hand froze before he touched the play button. The heavy curtain was an excellent sound barrier, but he didn't know how effective it would be against the music. Often he heard music through the walls of his apartment when he was trying to sleep. Since he kept such an irregular schedule, he didn't have the right to ask his neighbors to turn their music down, especially during the day when most people were at work. They probably weren't even aware when he was home, since he was there so seldom. He suspected that, despite the claims of the salesman as to the soundproofing quality of the curtain, it still wasn't as good a sound barrier as a wall. He tried to recall if he'd heard music in the background when Gwen was driving and he was sleeping. He hadn't heard a thing, but he didn't know if that was because she had had it on so quiet or if he'd slept that heavily. Somehow he doubted she'd put the music on at all.

He made a mental note to test exactly at what volume they could have the music playing when driving so as not to disturb whoever was sleeping at the time. He felt guilty now knowing that Gwen had driven most of the night in the boring silence.

Since Lionel had agreed to not touch the curtain once it had been closed, he left the music off, leaving him with only his thoughts for company.

On any trip, he thought about a lot of things while he drove, some important, some not. This time he could think only of Gwen. He wasn't sure he liked that.

For the past few years he hadn't thought much about women. After his experience with Sharon, he knew he would never get married, and because of his unpredictable schedule, he seldom dated. Except for the few times he wanted a little female companionship, there was no point.

Now he had no choice but to spend days and days with a woman he'd just barely met. Nothing would have adequately prepared him for this. The only consolation was that Gwen couldn't have foreseen this happening either and was equally caught off guard.

All was silent from behind, making him wonder if she was sleeping well. He didn't know if he would be able to hear the slight creaking of the bunk when she moved, but since he heard nothing, he assumed she was sleeping soundly.

Lionel frowned and focused his attention on the road. The only thing that should concern him was that she be well rested in order to drive safely.

He thought back to their previous conversations. In that short space of time, he'd seen many sides of Chad's niece. She had an easy sense of humor, yet there was nothing funny about the way she confronted those morons who had all but accused her of being a truck stop lizard. She had demonstrated a confidence and strength of character he didn't see often in a man or woman. She had shared her faith in the strangest way he'd ever seen, but he had a feeling that, one day, her words would come back to at least one person in that room, and the firmness of her conviction could make a difference.

Even though she had only taken up driving a truck on a dare, she showed no lack of respect for the profession. Instead, she treated him as an equal, despite the differences in education level between her years of university to obtain her teaching degree and his own education of barely passing high school. He had judged her unfairly, assuming that just because she was a woman, she couldn't do the job.

He was wrong. The woman had moxie. She wasn't a bad driver, either. And she was adapting well to life on the road.

He continued to drive in quiet, checking his watch more often than he ever did before, wondering how long she needed to sleep. Finally, after six hours and forty-seven minutes of driving alone, the rasp of the Velcro sounded behind him.

"Hi," he said, knowing he was smiling much more than he should have been. "Sleep well?" A sign ahead indicated a rest stop coming up, so he began to slow down.

She smiled back as she slid into the seat and buckled her seat belt. He forced his attention to the road.

"Yes, I did. I must have been more tired than I thought. I didn't hear a thing. That bunk is much softer than I figured it would be. I was out like a light. It sure feels strange to be waking up at this time. I feel like eating breakfast, but it's nearly supper time."

"Most truck stops have bacon and eggs on the menu 'round the clock."

She scrunched up her nose, which on a woman should have been cute, but when Gwen did it, she only looked miffed at his suggestion. "That's too greasy. I like something more healthy for breakfast."

"Don't start that again."

Gwen laughed but didn't comment.

Lionel pulled into the stop without being asked. Her little smile as she ran out of the truck for the amenities building did something funny in his stomach, but he passed it off as not having eaten for a while. When she returned, he was already digging into the fridge.

"Let's eat now," he said. "I think I'm hungry, too."

Lionel made coffee while Gwen carried the bag of sandwiches to the picnic table. She didn't comment on the lack of tableware, and briefly he considered teasing her about it, but when they stopped to pray, he no longer felt like fooling around.

They ate in silence, and Lionel didn't miss the conversation. He felt comfortable with her, more comfortable than he'd felt with anyone in many, many years. They didn't need words.

They both chose the same moment to stand, clean up the mess, and return to the truck. Lionel drove only as far as the next truck stop, where they fueled the truck. When they were done, they went inside the restaurant for a cup of coffee. The sun was setting, and from here they would be driving most of the night without stopping, except to switch drivers.

Lionel sat back, cradling the cup in his palms as Gwen pulled a scrap of paper out of her pocket then plopped her purse on the table. She pulled out a calculator, a ruler, a pencil, and her driving logbook, then started writing. She checked back and forth from the paper to the logbook, drawing little dots and making notes in the logbook. She then used the ruler to draw perfectly straight lines joining the dots.

He finally couldn't stand it. "What are you doing?"

She didn't look up as she pressed one finger on the page and dutifully added up all her figures. "I'm doing my logbook."

"With a ruler and a calculator?"

She still didn't look up. "I strive for accuracy," she mumbled as she wrote down the total, then began to add the next column.

He peeked over at the volumes of notes she'd made, then shook his head. "You don't need to write all that stuff down. They don't need to know exactly how much time it took to fuel, how long it took you to eat, what you dreamed about, or anything else I'd rather not discuss. All you need to have in there are your driving hours, the hours you've worked but weren't driving, off-duty hours, and time sleeping. Four things. That's all they need to know."

"I want to do this. Like a journal."

He opened his mouth to protest but snapped it shut again. Teachers probably did stuff like that all the time; it was probably second nature for her. Out on the road it wouldn't be very long and she would see such detail was unnecessary.

She pulled a separate piece of paper out of the back of her logbook, also scribbled with notes. "So up until now, you've driven eight hours and fifteen minutes, and I've driven nine and a half in this twenty-four-hour period."

"You've figured out *my* driving time in *your* logbook?"

"This is pretty calculated, you know. It's not as easy as driving a total of twenty hours, leaving a window of four hours that the truck doesn't move. It's different when you have to figure that once each of us has driven ten hours, we have to rest for eight in between. We can't have an overlap where there won't be an eight-hour break between the last time someone drove with the other having enough driving hours to fill the break. If that happens, the truck can't move."

She added a few more numbers to the paper. "So if you drive one and three-quarter hours tonight, that ends your legal allotment for the day. I have half an hour left, but that will bring us to midnight, where I can start on the next twenty-four-hour period, so I can keep driving. I've had my eight-hour break, and you haven't."

Lionel shook his head and stared at her. He hadn't ever gone into such detail. He'd never needed to.

She frowned and started to draw a table on the same page. "I figure I can draw up a schedule so we can actually get twenty hours of driving between the two of us in each twenty-four-hour period, including the eight-hour breaks between, fueling the truck once a day like you said, and eating and personal time, and do it quite comfortably."

"You're drafting up a schedule?"

She slid the paper across the table and pointed to a chart with that day's date and the times written down until that moment. "We can stay here in the restaurant for another half hour." She snapped the book shut, laid her pencil down, and smiled ear to ear. "So that means we can relax and have dessert. I'm having a piece of that great-looking peach pie in the front case. With ice cream."

Lionel didn't comment. He'd never relaxed on schedule before. He ordered a chocolate donut.

five

Gwen settled into the passenger seat and clicked on her seat belt. Lionel hadn't seemed too impressed with her attempts at making a schedule. But it was the only way she knew to accomplish the maximum allowable driving time while they had such a critical load. She would have thought that since a trucker had to live by a schedule, he'd be used to such things. Apparently not.

He didn't speak until they'd reached highway speed, and then his voice startled her. "I've been thinking."

Gwen cringed. She should have felt this coming. They hadn't even spent one day together and already it wasn't going to work. She stiffened her back and turned to look at him as he drove. She could see his profile in the lights of the dash. Out of nowhere the thought struck her what a handsome man he was. Not only that, but he'd been helpful and considerate. Every nice thing Uncle Chad had said about him was right. She quickly erased those thoughts from her mind as she cleared her throat. "Yes?"

"When I drive at night I usually have the music or the radio on, or even in the daytime when there's no one to talk to. It helps fight the boredom of the long stretches. The curtain is supposed to be really soundproof. We should test it with the music and see if we can have it on without disturbing each other."

Gwen blinked. "Uh. . .sure. . ." She glanced behind her at the bunk. Since they had known Lionel would be the next one to have a sleep, they had tucked her sleeping bag underneath, and his blankets and pillow were piled in the corner of the bunk, ready for him. She didn't want to go there.

Gwen mentally kicked herself. If she was scared of getting

in the same area as a pile of blankets, she had to have a screw loose. Without another word, she climbed into the bunk, flicked on the small light, closed the curtain, and listened.

His muffled voice drifted through the curtain. "Can you hear that?"

The constant hum of the motor was louder than the music, because she couldn't hear a thing. "No!" she called back.

She waited a few seconds and he called out again. "How about now?"

This time she could actually hear it. It was still soft enough that it wouldn't keep her awake. "You can make it louder. It's still okay."

This time she could almost make out the words, and that would disturb her. However, she didn't want to be unrealistic. If this arrangement was going to work, she couldn't infringe too much on his routine, and that included the volume at which he played his music.

Gwen glanced to the pile of blankets in the corner of the bunk.

She tended to sleep completely bundled up and liked to have the corner of her blanket or, in this case, sleeping bag, tucked under her chin and over her ears, no matter what time of year. Because of that, she'd always had difficulty sleeping in the summer heat. Despite the summer heat, she couldn't sleep with her ears uncovered. She didn't know why she did it, but she couldn't remember ever sleeping any other way. A completely unexpected bonus of her temporary summer job was that the truck was air-conditioned, so she found sleeping comfortable. She'd slept better last night in the truck than she had in the past month.

The only way to know if the music would disturb her would be to lie down as if she were about to really sleep.

Very slowly she unfolded Lionel's blanket. She wasn't going to wrap herself in his personal blanket, but she did lie down and pull just the corner of it over under her chin and over her cheek and ear, as if she were going to go to sleep.

She could still hear the music, but it would never prevent her from falling asleep. Gwen closed her eyes and snuggled her face into the fuzzy fabric and tried to imagine that she was really ready to fall asleep. It wasn't difficult. The blanket was thick and soft, not what she figured a man's blanket would be. Besides the soothing feel of the blanket against her face, it held a faint, spicy, male fragrance.

Gwen smiled. She liked this fragrance, and it was familiar to her, even though she couldn't remember from where. At first she considered that she might have dated a man who wore the same thing. She inhaled it again, then sat up with a start as she realized what it was. She'd smelled this scent from her brother's sleeping bag when she'd borrowed it. Garrett was a very basic kind of guy, not into cologne or other trappings. What she was smelling wasn't cologne, it was deodorant.

She pushed the blanket away and hurriedly folded it up as she called through the curtain. "That's fine. If I was lying down to sleep, that wouldn't bother me at all."

Once everything was neatly back in the corner, she parted the curtain and slid back into the passenger seat, grateful that, in the dark, he couldn't see the blush she knew was on her cheeks.

"I had that on volume level eleven. Are you sure that wouldn't bother you?"

Heat spread into her cheeks even more as she nodded quickly. "Positive."

"Well, if you're sure."

Gwen turned her head, studying whatever was out the window, even though it was pitch black and she couldn't see a thing. "I'm sure."

They continued to chat about nothing in particular until Lionel's allowable driving time was up. He pulled into the next rest area, but instead of just switching drivers, they decided to go for a walk and stretch their legs.

The rest area was deserted. The moon was almost full, so even with no artificial lighting except for the lights shining from the window of the amenities building, the picnic area was not in total blackout.

Gwen tapped Lionel on the arm. "Want to jog around?"

His little grin made crinkles appear in the corners of his eyes. "Do better than that. Race ya." He took off laughing and without saying, "Go."

Years of competing with Garrett had conditioned Gwen to shift into high gear instantly. Lionel hadn't gone far before she bolted after him.

She caught up quickly, but when she did, he quickened his pace, which forced her to speed up, too. She caught up to him again, but he ran faster still. Gwen ran for all she was worth, and by the time they neared the end of the circular path around the area, she was ahead of him.

She raised her hands in the air as they crossed the imaginary finish line where they began, beside the truck. "I won! I beat you!" she gasped.

Lionel stood still and bent at the waist, resting his hands on his knees for a few seconds before he straightened. "Whew!" he panted. "I'm more out of shape than I thought."

Gwen shook her head while she also struggled to catch her breath. "Me, too. I'm not used to this anymore."

Without any further discussion, they walked around the path once again as their breathing and heart rates slowed to normal. Then they hopped back into the truck, this time with Gwen in the driver's seat.

After driving a while, Gwen couldn't hold back a giggle. "I suppose I should tell you that I jog around the field before school twice a week with my students to keep in shape. And our jog often turns into a race. I don't always win."

His answering smile quickened her heartbeat, even though their race was long over. "I suppose I should tell you that I sit all day."

"Well, still, you didn't do too bad for someone so old and out of shape."

His hands went to his stomach, which, from what Gwen had previously seen, was not the least bit out of shape. "I'm not that bad. I do make an effort to get some exercise. And I'm not that old, I'm only thirty-one!"

"Well, I'm thirty, and I beat you."

"Let's see if you can beat me on the last day of summer, after you've been driving for two months. I think that's enough time to lose that edge. And you *will* lose it."

Gwen opened her mouth to issue a challenge but snapped it shut before she spoke. A situation exactly like this had gotten her into this mess in the first place. Only, for something that was such a mess, she really was enjoying herself.

Lionel turned the radio on and they rode without conversation, until he yawned. "I think not getting enough sleep is catching up with me. I'm tired. If you don't mind, I'm going to crawl into the back."

She shook her head. "Not at all. Good night."

When the curtain closed behind her, Gwen turned the music down to a level slightly lower than what Lionel had said when they tested it earlier. After a few songs, she hadn't heard from him asking her to turn it down, so she assumed he was able to fall asleep without difficulty.

This time she was more relaxed driving alone in the night, although driving through the flatlands of Colorado instead of through the mountains at night might have something to do with it. She enjoyed the music and was pleased to see that many of the CDs in his collection were also her favorites.

At sunrise Gwen pulled into a truck stop, but this time Lionel poked his head out before she left the truck. "Sleep well?" she asked.

He mumbled something that might have been a yes, and Gwen tried to stifle her smile.

"What's so funny?" he grumbled as he sat on the edge of

the bunk to tie the laces on his sneakers.

"Are you always crabby in the morning?"

"I'm not crabby. The light's too bright."

They walked together into the building but parted ways as soon as they entered. As soon as Gwen sat at the table, she made a note of the time in her logbook, then pulled out the novel she'd half-read and ordered a coffee while she waited for Lionel.

She read a whole chapter by the time he joined her, and again all traces of his earlier mood were gone. His hair was combed and slightly damp, he'd shaved, and he wore new clothes.

"Later today when we stop and fuel, I've got to do laundry. This is the last of my clean stuff. Remember, I didn't make it home after my last trip; they dispatched me straight out."

She hadn't thought about doing laundry. After her first trip with Uncle Chad, they'd had a couple of days at home, and even though she didn't do much other than laundry and make a number of phone calls the first day, she didn't think about the possibility that she might have to do laundry away from home.

Another good thing about being single and living at home was that she didn't have to worry about coming home to an empty fridge. When she got back, her mother had made a feast for dinner and then invited not only Garrett and Robbie but also Molly and Ken. As expected, Molly nattered on and on about what a dumb idea it was for her to be driving all summer. Gwen had passed off the remarks, but now, when it was too late to do anything about it, she could acknowledge that, even though she'd had a nice enough time with Lionel, the bottom line was, Molly was right. She was crazy for doing this.

Lionel ordered bacon and eggs, which was fine for him because it was breakfast and it was, after all, six in the morning. However, Gwen had been driving for seven hours, and she was famished.

The waitress didn't bat an eyelash, but Lionel nearly choked on his coffee when she ordered a hamburger and fries with all the trimmings. She waited for him to comment, but he didn't. It was almost like he was testing her by *not* saying anything, and that by doing so, he was goading her into starting something. She refused to take the bait.

This time they didn't linger. As soon as they were finished eating, they climbed back into the truck, ready to roll. They needed to save their non-driving time for later so Lionel could do his laundry.

Gwen liked the early morning best of all. It was nearing the end of Lionel's eight-hour break, and even though the meal helped refresh her, she was more than ready for a long break. She needed to relax.

As she continued to drive, an eagle soared overhead. The sunrise had been beautiful, but now that it was daylight, she wanted to take in the beauty of the fields and meadows on either side of the highway and take some pictures. During her short time as a trucker, she'd already seen many different kinds of birds and animals, including a fox or something at the side of the road a few miles back. From time to time, cute little gophers scampered across the highway.

"It sure is pretty in the morning," she sighed. "Everything is so fresh, the heat of the day hasn't made the birds and animals seek shelter yet."

Lionel raised one finger in the air and leaned back in his seat. "There are animals out at night, too. You just don't see them."

"Yes, I have. Last night I saw a couple of deer at the side of the road. Their eyes caught the headlights and they froze when the light was on them, just like the textbooks said they did."

"I didn't mean the deer. In some parts you'll see moose, too, by the way. I was talking about other critters. Snakes and lizards and things that go bump in the night."

She turned her head, gave him a big fake toothy smile, then

turned back to the road. "Don't try to frighten me by talking about bats and bugs and stuff. They don't scare me, so don't bother wasting your time. My brother is a forest ranger, and you wouldn't believe the animals and creepy crawlies he's been so kind to show me over the years."

He grinned back. "I had to try. So unseemly creatures don't scare you. Big, loud-mouthed truckers don't scare you. Tell me, what does scare you?"

Gwen shrugged her shoulders. "I don't know. Lots of things." One thing that was scaring her right now was Lionel, even though there was nothing big or loud-mouthed about him, nor did he have scales or smell bad. He made her feel comfortable, which in itself wasn't a bad thing, but he made her feel *too* comfortable. There were times they didn't need words, they knew what the other was thinking and acted accordingly. The only person she'd ever experienced that connection with was her brother, and that wasn't the same. They were twins, and over the years she'd learned that the bond she shared with Garrett was unique.

She didn't know anything about Lionel beyond what Uncle Chad had told her and what she'd learned herself in the past couple of weeks. And now, traveling across the continent with a man she barely knew, she should have been frightened, or at least nervous. Instead, beyond the few awkward moments she knew would happen, she trusted him completely. And she shouldn't have. She felt comfortable around him. And that made her nervous.

"What scares me is one of the kids in my Sunday school class. I teach grades eight and nine from Monday to Friday, but on Sundays I got the grade fives this year. There's one boy in the class who I think spends his spare time dreaming up the next bizarre thing he's going to do when he gets to church. Last month he came with his hamster in his pocket. I put it in a box so I could teach the class without the distraction, but the critter chewed its way out. And the worst part was, after we caught it and put it in a hamster-proof container, he made me promise not to tell his parents about what he'd done so he wouldn't get in trouble."

"What did you do?"

"I know his parents fairly well, and it was something they should have known, but I couldn't tell because I promised. I'm his Sunday school teacher, and I have to be an example to him, which means not betraying a confidence."

"That's a tough one."

"But I got him back." Gwen laughed, in spite of herself. "I made him write a note of thanks to everyone who helped catch his hamster. And then the parents of the children who received the notes phoned his mother to say how nice Jeremy was for doing that." She laughed again. "But I didn't say a word to anyone about the escapist hamster. He still doesn't know how his parents found out."

He pretended to shudder. "Remind me never to hold you to a promise." Gwen knew he was smiling, but even knowing that, she turned to acknowledge his unstated approval.

"So tell me, what else has he done to you that he scares you so much?"

She opened her mouth to continue when another little gopher ran onto the road ahead of them. But instead of running all the way across, he stopped in the middle of the highway, directly on the center line, and sat up on his cute little behind and looked straight at the truck bearing down on him.

At the speed at which the truck was moving, she knew the turbulence as she passed would knock him off his little bottom and send him rolling on the pavement, which would probably hurt him. Gwen turned the wheel slightly and aimed the truck to hug the shoulder line so she could pass him as far away as possible. Suddenly, the gopher decided to run. Instead of going back the way it had come, it ran to her side, directly in front of the truck.

"No!" she called out. "Not that way, little fella!"

Gwen felt a bump.

Lionel muttered something nasty under his breath.

Gwen's stomach rolled. She tightened her grip on the wheel, and her eyes started to burn.

"I hate when that happens," Lionel mumbled. "You'd think they would. . ." His voice trailed off.

She knew he was looking at her. She refused to turn her head. The burn in her eyes worsened, and her hands started to feel shaky.

"Gwen?"

She swallowed hard. "I used to feed them at the zoo when I was a kid." Her chin quivered. She clenched her teeth but she couldn't stop it.

He mumbled something else she couldn't hear. "Pull over," he said, more loudly.

She quickly swiped at her nose with the back of her hand, then grabbed the wheel again, holding it much tighter than she needed to. She choked the words out, trying to keep her voice steady. "We can't stop here."

"Yes, we can. That's what the shoulder is for. Pull over."

She needed to be tough. She wanted to show him that she could act like a professional. People ran over gophers all the time on the flatlands. She had to show him that she could be strong, even though she'd just murdered one of God's innocent woodland creatures with twenty tons of mobile machinery. The poor little thing hadn't had a chance.

Gwen's vision blurred, and she couldn't blink it away. One tear trickled down her cheek.

Gwen pulled over.

The second they were at a stop, before Lionel had a chance to undo his seat belt, she dashed straight for the bunk. "I'm really sleepy. I don't think I need to wind down. Good night."

And she whipped the curtain shut.

six

Lionel stared at the closed curtain, his mouth wide open, the words not having had a chance to leave his mouth. His hand still rested on the seat belt clip. He hadn't had enough time to press the button and release it.

She'd moved faster than the truck ever had, and the closed status of the curtain was as effective as a fortress wall.

He'd run over many gophers in his career as a driver, and it was still upsetting when it happened to him. Most of the other drivers joked about it, trying to out-macho each other, but he knew he wasn't the only one who felt bad when it happened. He wanted to tell her that, but she'd run off before he could say a word. And now she was sequestered behind the curtain, which he'd promised never to touch.

Not that he knew what to do with a crying woman, but he wanted to do something. One thing he did know. He didn't want to sit and stare at the curtain while she cried. He couldn't hear her, but he knew what she was doing. He'd never felt so helpless in his life.

Lionel slid into the driver's seat and turned the radio on. As soon as he reached the speed limit, he flipped on the cruise control.

He had nothing to do but drive and listen to the music.

Things had gone so well until this point, although nothing had gone like he expected. He could understand that she was upset about running over the gopher, but it bothered him that she'd shut him out and not allowed him the opportunity to help her deal with it.

He'd counted on, and even looked forward to, the next few hours, wanting to enjoy the morning, talking to her as he drove, before she crawled into the bunk for a sleep. Instead, he was alone in the driver's seat again, and she was in the back crying.

As the miles rolled by, he tried to think of something he could say when she got up. Besides the standard rhetoric that it happened to every driver at some point, the best he could come up with was to tell her there was nothing anyone could do to avoid them. She probably wouldn't derive much comfort from being told that, in the eyes of the company or an owner operator who had his life's savings tied up in his truck, risking an accident wasn't worth a little gopher. Nor did he think she'd get much consolation if he told her to be grateful it wasn't something bigger, like a moose, that she'd hit.

He remembered a few years back when one of his friends hit a moose outside of Thunder Bay. Thankfully the driver hadn't been badly hurt, but the truck had sustained heavy damage and the trailer had gone over into the ditch on impact. The weight of the load had busted out the roof of the trailer, and it had taken an entire crew three days of picking through the muddy, stagnant water to recover everything. Then it took a year and a half for the head office to settle all the damage and loss claims. Very few people realized that much of the cost of an accident wasn't covered by insurance, which made the company not look favorably on accidents caused by wildlife.

By noon she still hadn't appeared. Lionel tried to convince himself that it wasn't a major deal because she'd been in the bunk for only four hours and she was due for a sleep anyway. When his stomach grumbled, he stopped at a truck stop, pulling into an area of the parking lot he thought would be the quietest. Leaving the motor running so the roar of it wouldn't disturb her when he started it again, he dashed into the building, bought a sandwich and a coffee, and ran back. Since the curtain remained closed, he ate his lunch alone as he drove.

❧

By mid-afternoon Lionel thought he must have checked his watch a couple of hundred times. He was beginning to wonder if she would ever come out, when the rasp of the Velcro sounded.

He purposely kept his focus straight ahead. "Good morning, stranger. Sleep well?" he asked, then kicked himself. By being too cheerful he didn't want her to think that he knew she'd been doing anything other than sleeping.

"Yes, thank you." She slid into the passenger seat.

No words passed between them as he drove. He pulled into the first rest area and hopped out of the truck to catch a breath of fresh air when she went into the amenities building.

He waited as she tossed her purse up into the truck. "Want to go for a walk before we get moving again?"

She nodded but didn't comment so he started walking, expecting her to follow, which she did.

This time the silence bothered him. He had so many things to say but didn't know how to start. The things he felt he should say jumbled with what he wanted to say but couldn't, until he couldn't tell one from the other. Lionel decided to keep quiet.

"Uncle Chad told me it would probably take a while to get used to sleeping in a moving truck. He said some drivers never sleep well, that he and Jeff sleep and drive in five-hour shifts. But I haven't had any trouble sleeping."

"Me neither."

"And I'm really sorry, it's after three o'clock, and I didn't let you get into the fridge. You must be starving."

Lionel grinned. "I stopped and grabbed a quick sandwich at a truck stop. I couldn't believe it when you slept through. After all, there was food involved."

She shot him a dirty look, but he kept his gaze fixed forward and bit his bottom lip to stop himself from smiling. She continued when he pretended not to notice her scathing glare. "That's not all that surprising. I was really tired because I didn't get enough sleep the day before. Or the night before. Or whatever you call it when you sleep these strange hours."

He shrugged his shoulders. "I've never really thought about it. It's something you just get used to."

"Or not."

"I suppose. Are you hungry? If you want to make a quick snack, that's fine, but I really have to do some laundry, so we have to allow for a long stop at the next truck stop. That will have to be our real supper break, while we're waiting for the washing machine and stuff."

"I just woke up. I don't want supper."

He laughed, letting himself relax, grateful that everything appeared to be all right, after all. "Right. You're the one who had a hamburger and fries for breakfast."

"That wasn't breakfast. That was supper at six in the morning. Now it's time for breakfast at," she checked her wristwatch, "three forty-seven in the afternoon."

This particular rest area was much smaller than the one they'd stopped at the day before, so they found themselves finishing their walk around the picnic area in a very short time. They were about to leave the grassed area and return to the parking lot when they heard a child squeal with delight.

"Mommy! Mommy! He took it!"

"Don't move, sweetie. Mommy wants to take your picture."

They watched a woman crouch down to take a picture of a little girl feeding bread to a black squirrel beside one of the tables.

Lionel's gut clenched at the sound of Gwen's sudden intake of breath. He remembered her comment that, as a child, she'd enjoyed feeding the gophers at the zoo. He had a bad feeling that she was thinking of a gopher that wouldn't ever get fed again.

He grabbed her hand. "Let's go. We don't want to get behind schedule. You know all about schedules."

She stiffened but allowed him to lead her to the truck.

He fished in his pocket for the keys. "You want to drive or ride?"

Her voice, when she answered, wavered slightly. "Either way, whatever you want."

He stuffed the keys back into his pocket and grasped both her hands. "Gwen, I know you're upset about it. It's okay to be upset. Even us guys feel bad when we hit an animal. Even little ones like gophers."

Being at virtually the same height, she seemed closer than she really was. If she were shorter, it would have given him some distance as she stared at him with those big round eyes—eyes that started to well up with tears. She blinked a few times and the moisture cleared.

He dropped her hands and slid his palms up to her shoulders, which probably wasn't very smart, because it only drew her closer. The softness of her hair as it brushed his fingers made him want to run them through the dark locks. Her hair was an unusual color, a brown so dark it was almost black, and even though she hadn't had a shower in two days, it still looked fresh. It shone in the afternoon sunshine with a natural luster he thought would have looked good in a shampoo commercial. He knew he shouldn't be touching her hair, or any part of her, but he couldn't move away.

"You probably think I'm such a ninny. I know it was just a gopher. It's not like it was someone's dog or anything."

He wound his fingers in her hair, amazed at the silky feel of it. "You're not a ninny."

He spread his fingers and watched as her hair slipped between them, and then returned his attention to her beautiful chocolate brown eyes. As soon as they made eye contact, she bit her bottom lip, her eyes grew moist, welled up, and overflowed.

"Aw, nuts. . ." he mumbled. He pulled her forward, and when she didn't resist, he surrounded her with a hug. At her height, her chin rested exactly on top of his shoulder as they stood. She sniffled again, right beside his ear, sending a feeling of dread through him that she was going to start sobbing her guts out, right in the parking lot.

Now he really didn't know what to do.

Very gently he rubbed small circles on her back, doing his best to soothe her. She didn't cry but, instead, let go a ragged sigh. The tension in her shoulders relaxed beneath his touch, so he didn't stop. Lionel closed his eyes. A few strands of her hair tickled his nose. Instead of turning his head away, he pressed his cheek into her hair.

He knew what he wanted to do. He wanted to kiss her. Very slowly he began to turn his head until his whole face was buried in her hair. All he had to do was touch her chin with his fingertips to turn her head just a little and he would be in just the right position.

At the realization of what he was about to do, his eyes bolted open. He backed up about an inch, creating some distance between them. As soon as he pulled away, Gwen also stiffened and backed up, completing the separation.

She swiped her eyes with the back of her hand and sniffled. "Thanks, I feel better now. We've got to get going, we've got miles to make."

ஐ

Gwen started to slow the truck as they approached the exit for the truck stop, noting the time on the dashboard clock. "I've driven for nine hours today, you've driven for seven. We've already used two hours of non-driving time, but we can still get in ten hours each for this twenty-four-hour period if we hurry. Tell me all that we need to do, in case I've forgotten something."

Lionel checked his watch. "We have to fuel and do our trip fuel sheets, and update our personal fuel log as well as our trip logbooks. While we're stopped and we still have daylight we should clean the clearance lights and windows and check the tires. Plus you want to have a shower, and I have to do my laundry. Oh, and we were going to have supper. We'll never do it."

Gwen tilted up one corner of her mouth while she downshifted, organizing the details and guesstimating how long each step would take. Lionel opened his mouth while she was still thinking, so she quickly shook her head to silence him in order to take a few more seconds to calculate her plan. She turned her head for a second to catch his attention. "We can do it if we organize ourselves efficiently."

"Oh, yeah. Right," he grunted, and crossed his arms over his chest.

Gwen slowed their speed to a crawl and rolled up to the pump. "We can do this." She applied the hand brake, but before she released the seat belt, she grabbed a pen and a napkin from the slot and calculated how long each duty would take as she wrote the details of her plan. "You begin fueling, I'll start the laundry and reserve the shower. While I'm doing that, you clean the windows." She stuck her tongue out of the corner of her mouth as she figured out how long the washer would run and tried to recall how long the fueling and maintenance took them yesterday. "When everything is in the washer, I'll come back and do the clearance lights and tires. Then I'll go have my shower. You'll be finished with the fueling and the windows by the time I'm done, and by then the washer should be finished. We can throw everything in the dryer and then go have supper. We can do the paperwork while we eat. By the time we're finished the clothes should be dry, then we can move out."

He didn't speak, so she handed him the napkin as proof that she was right.

"Come on, Lionel, we don't have much time."

"I don't believe this." He looked down at her notes on the crumpled napkin. "I'm traveling with the Schedule Queen."

Gwen reached across the space between the seats and poked him in the arm. "Trust me. This will work."

He handed the napkin back. He spoke so softly she could barely make out what he said. "You missed calculating how many seconds it would take for me to brush my teeth."

She glared at him and crossed her arms over her chest. "Did you say something?"

"Nothing worth repeating," he grumbled as he unclipped his seat belt then reached for the door handle.

Gwen loudly cleared her throat, making him freeze in place. She purposely didn't say anything but narrowed her eyes and gave him her best dirty look, one she'd perfected on her brother.

He raised his palms in the air toward her and sighed. "Okay, I give up. I'll do it your way."

Gwen immediately stepped into the back and pulled out her bag of dirty laundry. "Where's your stuff?"

He opened the door and started to leave but stopped at her question, leaving one leg sticking out as he answered. "The rags are in the bin underneath where your clothes are, like they usually are."

"No, not that. I meant your clothes. The stuff you need washed."

"Oh, that's in a bag in the bin on the bottom left. It's. . ." His voice trailed off. The door closed, but instead of being outside to start fueling the truck, he appeared beside her in the cab. "I'll do the laundry."

Gwen stiffened and tightened her grip on her own laundry bag. She didn't want a man going through her personal things. "It's okay, I can do it. You go fuel the truck."

He shook his head and pulled a bag out of the bin he'd told her to check, but didn't give it to her. "You fuel the truck. I'll do the laundry."

They stood, neither one moving, staring at each other, neither giving up his or her bag of laundry.

Gwen bowed her head and pinched the bridge of her nose. "We don't have time for this. It's okay, Lionel. Really." She reached for the bag, but when she grasped it and started to pull, he didn't let go. Gwen squeezed her eyes closed. "Lionel, I assure you, you don't own anything I haven't seen before."

His cheeks reddened, but he still didn't let go.

She pulled a little harder. "I have a twin brother. I've washed a man's underw. . .uh. . .personal items before. It's not a big deal. Come on, we don't have time for this." It wasn't that she was anxious to do his laundry, but there was no way she was going to let him wash *her* underwear.

"As long as you promise to dump the load in the machine without looking."

"I promise. Now let go."

Reluctantly, he released his grip. While he was acting mildly complacent, Gwen hopped out of the truck and ran to the front counter to make the necessary arrangements.

On her travels with Uncle Chad, when they'd stopped at night she got a motel room, so she'd always had the comfort of her own bathroom, shower included. Then, in the morning when she was done with the room, she tidied up the truck while Uncle Chad had his shower. This was going to be her first experience with renting a truck stop shower.

She told herself that the facilities would be similar to those available at the various campsites she'd been to over the years. After she put her name down, she went into the truck stop's Laundromat, pulled a few pairs of jeans out of Lionel's bag, and stuffed them into the machine with her own jeans. Then she dumped everything else into another machine without looking, along with the few things of her own that needed washing, just as she'd promised.

She hustled back to the truck and quickly wiped off the clearance lights, walked around the unit to check the tires, then stood behind Lionel as he stood on the running boards, busily cleaning the windows.

"I'm going to have my shower now. Catch you in about twenty minutes." She retrieved her small overnight bag and some clean clothes out of the larger duffel bag and jogged to the shower area.

It wasn't exactly relaxing, but the shower left her feeling clean again, which she supposed was the point. She stuffed her toiletries back into her bag as she contemplated her last duty, that of transferring their clothes from the washer to the dryer. Then she would be meeting Lionel in the restaurant for supper.

Life on the road was vastly different from anything she'd ever experienced. Any other time she'd gone to a restaurant for dinner with a man she'd worn a skirt, a nice blouse, and, even though she usually didn't wear a lot of makeup, she always put some on when she went out on a date. She hadn't brought a single tube of lipstick with her for her truck-driving stint, and she certainly hadn't brought a curling iron.

Gwen peeked over her shoulder before she left the room and caught a glimpse of herself in the mirror. She paused, studying her image to see what everyone else saw.

Her hair was still damp and hung loosely to her shoulders. She wore no makeup, and her fine-dining attire was a T-shirt with the faded logo of a Christian summer camp where she'd counseled a few years ago. Her jeans were so well-worn the right knee almost had a hole. Her battered sneakers had seen better days, but they were the most comfortable she owned. She looked like a slob. A clean slob, but a slob just the same.

Not that she had to dress up for Joe's Truck Stop Cafe.

She imagined that this would be what married life was like—not having to care what she wore, coordinating dinner with a man in between work, laundry, cleaning, maintenance, and other chores. She ran her fingers through her hair to fluff it, and let it fall. No matter what she did, in her present state, nothing would improve.

While she was taking the classes for her Class-One license, a few friends had not-so-graciously pointed out that spending the summer trucking around the continent in her old clothes wasn't going to do anything for her single status. Everyone had only the best of intentions, but she was so tired of the well-meaning yet annoying attempts at matchmaking that she could hardly wait to get away, especially with the whole summer off. However, now that she was here in a hole-in-the-wall truck stop in the middle of the continent, she knew this wasn't what she had in mind.

So far her experiences on the road hadn't been bad, although she felt very sorry for Uncle Chad with his truck breaking down. She thanked God she hadn't been driving when it happened, because she knew, without any shadow of a doubt, that it wasn't her fault. However, she had been driving when that poor little gopher met its demise, and that was her fault. Except for killing the gopher, she was enjoying her summer so far.

Gwen slung her overnight bag over her shoulder and headed for the Laundromat. She transferred everything from the washers to the dryers and nearly bumped into Lionel in the doorway. "Great timing," she said. "You done?"

"Yes, are you?"

She nodded. It was suppertime, and not a minute too soon.

The second the waitress took their orders, Lionel spread a pile of papers and notebooks over the table. "This was a good idea. I think we really can do all this stuff in two hours and get in our full driving time. I'll do the fuel log and fuel trip sheets." He pushed both drivers' logbooks toward her. "Here. You can kill two birds with one stone, since you're so good at it." His hands froze, his eyes widened, and his face paled as he met her eyes. "I didn't mean that the way it sounded. I meant that you're good at making notes on my times in your logbook, so you can do both logbooks. Not that you're good at killing things. I meant doing two things at once. Like when—"

Gwen bit her bottom lip, reached over the piles of paper, and laid her hand over his, interrupting him before he dug himself in deeper. She really did appreciate his attempts to make her feel better. Lionel was really a sweet man, if one liked the loner type. "It's okay. I know what you meant. Let's get this paperwork cleared before the food comes."

seven

Lionel didn't bother to try to hide his smile. "Good morning. Or afternoon. Or whatever. Did you sleep well?"

She yawned as she flopped into the seat and clipped on her seat belt. "Yeah, I did."

Without needing to be asked, he prepared to stop at the first rest area or truck stop they came to, just as she'd done for him as soon as he woke up. It had been only a few days since they'd been driving together, but in those few days he suspected they had seen more of each other and done more talking than most married couples did in a month.

While he hadn't thought that they would argue, he had traveled alone for so many years that he had expected her constant companionship to get on his nerves. At the very least, he'd expected to do a lot of reading in the bunk to get away from her while she was driving, but he'd been in the bunk only to actually sleep.

Again, she'd driven all night while he slept, and then he'd driven until mid-afternoon while she slept. He tried not to feel guilty about Gwen driving the graveyard shift hours, but because Chad's breakdown happened when he was out of hours, it hadn't left them any leeway. Now they'd fallen into a pattern. While the hours she was driving were easiest for a beginner, with the least amount of traffic on the road, he knew that it wasn't fun to drive all night alone in the dark. He had also worried about how the change in her sleeping patterns would affect her, being up all night and sleeping in the early day, but she had adapted well.

Just like yesterday, he'd started getting antsy about noon, anticipating when she would wake up.

He checked the time. It was nearly three o'clock. "We'll be at Evansville before midnight. We've been making great time, and you've been doing real good. Are you sure you aren't going to be making a career change in September?"

"Not a chance. They need me at the high school, and the kids at church would miss me. I'd miss them, too. Besides, my sister-in-law is going to have a baby and I want to watch her grow big and round. I also have to laugh at Garrett every time he makes a fool of himself over the process of getting ready to become a father and going through the pregnancy with her. I can hardly wait for him to go to prenatal classes and watch all those ghastly films. It's my sisterly duty to remind him what he's in for."

"I'm sure he'll appreciate your efforts."

She smiled and stared off into nowhere in particular, making Lionel wish she could smile like that when she thought of him.

"He will, strange as it sounds. It wouldn't be right if I didn't. By the way, can I use your laptop? I have to send him an E-mail and see how they're doing. Robbie was going to have an ultrasound, and I think she's had it by now. I just want to make sure everything is okay."

"You know you can. You don't have to ask."

She turned her head and gave him a big smile.

He smiled back, his heartbeat quickened, and his chest swelled, knowing that this time her smile was for him.

Lionel cleared his throat and forced his attention back to the road. There was only one explanation for his sappy reaction to her simple gratitude. He was losing his mind.

He pulled into a rest area and waited inside the truck when she ran off to the amenities building, watching her every step until the door closed behind her. He couldn't believe that someone who ate so much could be so thin.

After this short stint was over and she was back with Chad, they would see each other only a few times when they crossed paths on the road or ended up back home at the Vancouver terminal at the same time, which wouldn't be often. After the summer was over, he would never see her again because she was going back to her teaching job, and he would continue with his life on the road.

He would be ten times a fool if he thought they could begin dating once life returned to normal. He'd been down that road before, and life had taught him well that it would never work. He had done his best to spend as much time as possible with Sharon when he wasn't away on the road. He had really thought they could be happy, because the time they spent together had been good, yet they weren't miserable when they were apart. The happiest day of his life had been the day she said she'd marry him. Up until that point, his relationship with Sharon had been everything his parents' relationship hadn't been.

Even though his father wasn't a trucker, his father traveled a lot for business. Looking back as an adult, he could see the progression of how his parents' marriage had failed, and he had vowed not to make the same mistakes.

When he was a kid he'd been witness to their many fights. He couldn't count the times as a child he'd hidden under his bed, praying to a God he really didn't know or understand to make the yelling stop. The screaming usually started the day before his father began his preparations to leave for yet another business trip. Even worse than the screaming matches, he'd had to endure his mother's constant complaints until his father returned, a mother telling her child what a jerk his father was and how his father didn't care.

He remembered when it stopped, which was when his mother found someone else.

The divorce was quick, but the custody arrangements had been painful. As he grew up, he'd avoided going home, because from Monday to Friday he had to listen to his mother correct everything he did so he wouldn't turn out like his father. Every weekend he'd had to listen to his father tell him what a selfish and ungrateful woman his mother was. Living with his mother on the weekdays and his father on the weekends, he'd had a difficult time making and keeping friends. He couldn't see his school friends on the weekends, because custody arrangements said that he lived at his father's house on the weekends, and his father insisted on his staying there all weekend. Then he couldn't see the few kids he'd met in his father's neighborhood during the week, because his mother wouldn't take him to his father's house on "her" time.

He would never do that to a child. Even before he became a Christian, Lionel promised himself that his marriage would be forever, and that no matter what troubles happened, he would do everything he could to make it work.

When he met Sharon, what attracted him the most was her independence. When they were apart she anticipated his return, but she had other things in her life to occupy her thoughts and her time. Both their lifestyles suited his being a trucker. They could function apart, and when they were together again, they were happy as well. As far as he could see, and according to what she told him, every time he left she missed him, but wouldn't pine for him, and eagerly awaited his return. A few weeks before what would have been their wedding date, he thought he'd surprise her when he'd been rerouted and come home early. The surprise had been on him. When he knocked on her door, she was with someone else.

He jumped at the sound of the truck door opening. Gwen hopped in and headed straight for the back. She rolled up her sleeping bag and raised and secured the bunk. She tucked her personal effects, including her overnight bag, into the bin they'd said would be hers, and pulled out his laptop computer. "I'm ready to go."

Lionel watched as she took her place in the passenger seat and fastened her seat belt. The woman was efficient and organized beyond belief. She was a good driver, yet she recognized her limitations as a beginner and was anxious to learn. When they stopped she did her share of the maintenance, even checking the oil. Still, doing what had, until recently, been considered a man's domain, she was every inch a woman. Even without makeup and in her wrinkled old clothes, Gwen Lamont was beautiful, inside and out. She had a heart of gold and a soul that radiated the love of Christ. One day some man would be lucky to have her.

Lionel found himself jealous of a man who so far didn't exist. He could have no future with her, he was realistic enough to see that. He knew enough not to enter into something that could never have a happy ending.

As he geared up the truck, she booted up the computer. While she waited for it, she gazed out the window and sighed. "It looks like this good weather is going to be over soon. When I was outside I could see big ugly gray clouds in the distance, and they're getting closer. I guess in this part of the country in the heat of the summer that means a thunderstorm is coming, doesn't it?"

"You never know. The clouds could disappear as quickly as they appear. Or we could miss it entirely. Actually, a little rain would be a nice break in this heat."

"Yes, it sure has been hot, way hotter here in Kansas than at home. Have I told you yet how grateful I am that your truck is air-conditioned?"

He grinned and quirked one eyebrow. "No. Tell me."

"I don't think I've ever slept so well in the heat of the summer. The air-conditioning is perfect when I. . ." Her voice trailed off. She lowered her head and began furiously typing her messages. "Never mind."

Lionel flipped on the cruise control when he reached cruising speed. Their pattern had been that he would drive for a couple of hours, then they would stop and fuel and eat. He would have an early supper, she would completely ignore his comments and have what she called a late breakfast, despite the time of day. Then she would drive for a few hours before he crawled into the bunk for a sleep. The pattern was comfortable, and it hadn't taken long to get used to.

As they continued eastward, the clouds in the distance billowed and expanded with a speed he'd never seen. In the blink of an eye, the sky became dark.

Gwen stopped typing and reached over to turn off the air-conditioning. "This is so strange. I don't like it, it's kind of scary. Does this happen often?"

A gust of wind rocked the truck.

"No, this doesn't happen often." He studied the clouds. Everything had happened too fast, and he didn't like it either. He also didn't like the sickly yellow-green color behind the gray of the clouds.

Another gust of wind hit the truck. "This isn't good, Gwen. Turn on the weather station."

Without question and without finishing what she was doing, she closed the laptop, laid it at her feet, and pushed the designated button on the radio that automatically zeroed in on the local weather station, no matter where in the continent they were.

A blast of hail pelted the truck at the exact second the announcer's voice came on the radio. Gwen turned up the radio in order to hear; the steady drone and bang of the hail nearly drowned out the voice.

". . .no funnel clouds have touched the ground so far, but Doppler radar indicates a severe line of thunderstorms accompanied by hail and heavy winds. Persons in the southwestern portion of the state should seek immediate shelter as it continues to travel northeast. I repeat, we have a tornado warning in the southwestern portion of the state. . ."

Lionel set the windshield wipers onto high. "We're in serious trouble like this in the middle of nowhere. Grab the map and see if there's an overpass nearby. We're sitting ducks out here."

A flash of lightning lit the sky, immediately followed by the crash of thunder directly above them. The hail instantly became so thick he couldn't see past the hood, pummeling the truck in fierce torrents, the ensuing onslaught battering the roof and hood in a deafening roar.

The truck started to slide. "Hang on!" he yelled over the din of the hail pounding them as he fought with the wheel. He struggled with all his strength to regain control. "And pray like you've never prayed before!"

He geared down and steered against the force of the wind and the hail as it pushed the truck. Until he could bring the unit to a full stop, they would continue to slide. Only when the truck was at a stop would they be safe, if he could do so before they toppled over in the ditch.

"I know you can do it," Gwen whimpered beside him, and then she started to pray.

He heard her, and he wanted to pray, too, but he had to pour all his energy and concentration into working against the wind, guessing where he was going, and trying to stop. If he touched the brake, the wheels would lock up, the truck would jackknife, and they would go over in the ditch.

He had no idea if there was anyone else on the road. It was the major interstate highway, and there would be other traffic besides them in the middle of the day, but he couldn't see where he was going or what he was doing. In the ten years he'd been driving, he'd never hit a snowstorm that blinded him as much as this summer hail. He wouldn't know if another car was on the road until he rode over it or hit it.

He frantically continued to gear down, fighting with himself not to touch the brake. After an eternity, when he was almost at a stop, he couldn't stand it anymore and stomped on the brake. The truck slid a few feet, shuddered, and settled with a jerk. Immediately he killed the motor and yanked on the parking brake.

Lionel turned to Gwen. Her face was pale, her eyes wide. "Don't move!" he called over the clanging of the hail. "Stay in the seat, and don't take off the seat belt!"

The falling hail outside the window surrounded them completely in a pasty gray void, but even in the dim, filtered light, he could see the fear in her. He'd never been so scared in his life either, but he knew that the safest thing to do was to remain seated, with the seat belt on.

"How do we know where the funnel is?" she yelled across the space between the seats.

"We don't."

She squeezed her eyes shut and pressed her folded hands to her heart, but she didn't touch her seat belt.

Lionel closed his eyes and prayed. For their safety. For the safety of those around them, *if* there was anyone around them. And mostly for Gwen, that no matter what happened, to him or the truck, she would be safe.

As suddenly as throwing a switch, all was quiet, except for the pounding of his heart.

Slowly Lionel opened his eyes. Within seconds the sky brightened and sunlight appeared. The wind stopped.

He looked outside.

The truck sat at an angle on the highway, blocking two lanes, the right rear tire of the trailer hovering over the edge of the ditch. Three inches of hailstones covered the ground, and mixed with the layers of hail, branches and tree limbs were strewn everywhere.

He checked around them for other vehicles. No one was in the ditch as far as he could see, but three cars were scattered as haphazardly across the highway as he was. All were upright.

"Looks like we caught only the outer edge. We're safe."

They both unfastened their seat belts at the same time and stood. His legs felt like they were made of rubber, but he couldn't stay in the seat a moment longer.

He met Gwen halfway between the seats. Lionel needed to touch her. To press her body close to his and hold her tight. To feel her heartbeat and, by experiencing the movement of her breathing against him, have the proof he needed to confirm that they were very much alive. But he didn't have that right.

His hands shook as he cupped her face.

Her eyes widened at his touch. Her voice was raspy and wavered as she spoke. "No flying cows out there?"

His own voice shook as he spoke, and he couldn't control it. "No, no flying cows."

He thought his heart had started to slow its pace, but when he felt the light touch of her fingers on his chest, pressing over his heart, he lost it.

Without a word or a thought of the consequences of his actions, he tipped her head and brought his mouth down on hers and kissed her for all he was worth. Her arms wrapped around his back, and all thoughts of why he shouldn't be doing this were forgotten. He kissed her with everything he had, from the bottom of his soul. And for the desperation with which he kissed her, she kissed him back in equal measure. He might have died and gone to heaven.

The muffled thud of a car door closing reminded Lionel that he was very much still on earth.

Very slowly he pulled back an inch, but only an inch and no more. If she pulled away from him, he thought his heart would surely tear in two. When she removed her hands from his back, he trailed his fingertips down her cheeks, keeping contact with her chin, needing to touch her, even in this small way. Instead of backing up, she rested her hands on his shoulders and, fortunately, remained silent, giving him the time he needed to think.

Lionel cupped her chin. Not moving, simply staring into her eyes, at that moment his heart said he loved her, but his head said it wasn't possible. His common sense said they were nothing alike, but his soul said she complemented him where he was weak, and he would support her when she needed someone to hold her up, as well.

He bent his head and brushed a short kiss to her lips, then released her.

Her face flushed and she backed up. "We'd better go outside and make sure everything's okay." In the space of two seconds, he was looking at the closed door, and he was alone inside his truck.

୬ୈ

Gwen walked through the puddles of water and melting hailstones. She stopped beside the back trailer tires, drew in a deep breath, pressed her palms against the trailer, and leaned her forehead against it as well. The cold of the metal wall soothed the heat from her face but did nothing to still her pounding heart or strengthen her wobbly knees.

He'd kissed her. And she'd kissed him back.

No one had ever kissed her like that before, and it had been scarier than the tornado. She hadn't seen the tornado, but she had more than felt its effects. Conversely, she had seen Lionel but didn't yet know the effects of what had happened between them. One thing she did know, Lionel Bradshaw was more dangerous than any tornado could ever be.

It was panic. Pure and simple.

Not that she would have kissed just anybody, tornado or not. She didn't understand the instant friendship that developed, but she was sure it had something to do with being with him almost nonstop, day and night. What she felt with Lionel confused her; it was different from anything she'd ever experienced, different from any relationship with any of her other friends, people she'd known for years. The immediate bond had thrown her, and panic made her respond.

There was no other explanation. She couldn't get involved with a trucker. She had a life and a routine to get back to, a life and a routine she knew and liked and was comfortable with.

After kissing her like that, Lionel left her feeling far from comfortable, and she didn't like it.

And now she had to go sit in the truck with him, not being apart from him unless one of them was sleeping, and pretend everything was okay.

Fortunately, they were near their destination, and soon they would be on their way home. By the time they were back to familiar territory, Uncle Chad's truck would be fixed, and life would be back to normal, or as normal as it could be, considering she'd never done anything like this before.

The thud of the truck's driver's door sounded. She peeked under the trailer to see Lionel hop off the running board and approach one of the three cars nearby. People had exited the other two, but no one had come out of the little red one.

A surge of dread coursed through her. Her first thought was that it might be an older person; perhaps someone had had a heart attack. She had certainly been more frightened than she'd ever been in her life, and the sheer weight of the truck had made it ten times safer than a car. She couldn't imagine what it would have been like for the other people.

She ran around the rear of the trailer and straight for the car.

Lionel opened the door before she arrived. She heaved a sigh of relief and skidded to a halt when instead of a person slumped over the wheel, inside was a woman clinging to two very frightened, screaming children.

Although she'd had some first aid training in her studies to become a teacher, she was much more comfortable handling crying children than sick or injured adults.

Because there were children, she wanted to take charge. Instead, Lionel coaxed the woman, a little boy, and a preschool-aged girl outside. The boy wouldn't let go of his mother's leg, but the little girl practically jumped into Lionel's arms, threw her arms around his neck, and sobbed freely while he stroked her hair.

A man from one of the other cars approached. "Radio says it's petered out. Nothing touched down, a few homes and buildings damaged, nothing completely destroyed, some minor injuries, no deaths."

"Praise the Lord," Lionel murmured into the little girl's hair.

The moisture had cooled the air somewhat, but the summer

sun and blue skies were back. If it weren't for the branches scattered on the ground, or the cars and truck helter-skelter on the highway, Gwen would never have been able to tell anything out of the ordinary had happened.

When the little girl was returned to her mother, Gwen and Lionel began their check of the air lines and tires before they resumed their journey. Not a word was spoken as they walked around the truck and trailer, falling into the same pattern they had every time they stopped, needing no elaboration.

Without asking, Gwen hopped through the driver's door and started the engine. "Well," she said as she engaged the clutch and threw the stick shift into first gear, "it's over. We made it."

Lionel grinned, a cute little boyish grin that quickened her heart, even though it shouldn't have.

"It's not over yet," he said. "After all that excitement, I have to visit the little boy's room."

Gwen groaned. Life on the road was a challenge in more ways than one.

eight

After she finished fueling the truck, Gwen parked it and walked into the restaurant.

When they had first pulled into the truck stop she had gently suggested that Lionel shower after all the tense moments. Instead of being embarrassed, he'd burst out laughing, made a rather bad joke, and told her that she'd have to fuel the truck and wash the windows herself. He had still been laughing when he walked into the truck stop office with his overnight bag slung over his shoulder, while all she could do was sit in the truck with her mouth hanging open.

She couldn't believe the things that passed as conversation between them. She didn't speak to her brother about the things she'd discussed with Lionel, yet she very much enjoyed the time she spent with him. There was only one explanation: She was losing her mind.

By the time she joined him in the truck stop's coffee shop, there were two cups of coffee on the table and Lionel was reading the menu.

"Finally. I thought I would starve to death by the time you got here."

Gwen refused to get into an argument about why women took longer to get dressed and ready than men. That was one of those many topics she didn't want to talk about with him but somehow always fell into. She slid into the chair and picked up the coffee cup, which he'd fixed just the way she liked it.

She took a slow draw on the coffee, savoring it, hardly able to believe that, after all that had happened in the few hours since she woke, it was only her first coffee of the day. Across the table, Lionel had nearly guzzled his entire cup. "You shouldn't be drinking coffee after all this," she mumbled over the cup. "You should be drinking something to calm yourself, like a nice soothing blend of herbal tea."

He closed both hands around his throat, crossed his eyes, and made a small gagging sound. A family seated at the next table turned to stare.

"Stop it," she ground out between her teeth. "You're embarrassing me."

"Herbal tea? What else do you think I should do, take up knitting? Or I know: needlepoint!"

Gwen sighed in exasperation. "I know a few men who knit. And it was only a suggestion."

He stopped the theatrics, leaned forward to rest his elbows on the table, and finished off the last of what was in the cup. "I was only fooling around, Gwen. You should know that by now."

The waitress returned with refills and took their orders, sparing her the need to comment. As had been their pattern, Lionel ordered supper fare and Gwen ordered a nice brunch, since for her it was the first meal of the day.

When the waitress left, Gwen watched Lionel take a long, slow sip of his second cup. The laughter had left his eyes, the moment had passed. They were on a mission, and it was time again to get on with life.

In contrast to his silly actions, when faced with a crisis his behavior was quite sober. He'd recovered quickly when thrust into the position of driving with her to take the critical load of machinery across the continent, especially considering the unusual circumstances in which they'd found themselves. His treatment of her while traveling together was beyond reproach.

His performance in the face of the tornado was exceptional. If she had been driving, she was positive she would have sent them over in the ditch. As it was, they were close. Her stomach clenched at the memory of the rear tire partly overhanging into the ditch. A few more inches and the trailer would have gone down, and then the whole truck, and them along with it. The way he'd comforted the hysterical child had almost brought her to tears.

Lionel was a nice man, and she thanked God she had been teamed up with him, for things could have been a lot worse. They both agreed that, no matter where in the country they were on Sunday morning, they would attend church together. If they weren't near a big city with a church that had parking facilities to accommodate the truck and trailer, then they would hopefully find a small truckers' chapel on the road wherever they were. Failing that, they had agreed to simply stop and have their own worship time, just the two of them, at the side of the highway, if necessary.

The clink of Lionel returning the cup to the saucer broke her out of her musings. "Actually, there is something I've got to talk to you about."

Gwen cringed. They'd talked about so much in the time they'd spent together. Some personal, some not. About family and preferences. Lifestyles. Their faith and beliefs. Considering the amount of time they'd been together, there wasn't much silence in the truck. They'd used the CB radio only a few times because they'd talked about so many interesting and important things, they didn't need the meaningless chatter with strangers.

Tonight they would be at their destination, and their critical trip would be at an end. She didn't like the serious tone of his voice, because it gave her a feeling he was going to tell her something she didn't want to hear.

"Why don't you ever use the cruise control? At first I could see why, what with you being a new driver and all, but really, it's great once you get used to it. I know it feels funny not using your feet when you drive, but it saves a lot on fuel. We would save money if you used the cruise control."

Cruise control? All she had been able to think about for the past few hours was the way he'd kissed her and how good she felt in his arms, what kind of person he was and the next few days of driving together. He was thinking about gas mileage?

Gwen shook her head. "You've got cruise control on your truck? You're kidding, right?"

"You didn't know? But I use it all the time. Certainly you've seen me engage it. Or Chad, when he uses his."

"Uncle Chad never showed me cruise control. I didn't know you could even get cruise control put on a truck."

"It was an option when I bought the unit, and it was a good decision."

"I've never noticed you turning it on. Or maybe I did and didn't realize what it was you were doing. I didn't know you'd be concerned about fuel economy in a big thing like that."

"Especially in a *big thing*," he emphasized the words, "like that. Driving a truck is a business, and it's important to minimize expenses. We go through two hundred and twenty gallons of diesel fuel a day. It's an expense that adds up quickly."

"Well, I think someone should invent a solar-powered diesel engine."

He shook his head at her inane statement. "Do you know what you just said?"

"You know what I meant."

He squeezed his eyes shut for a second. "Unfortunately, I think I'm getting used to it."

She wanted to ask what he meant, but the waitress delivered their meals. After a prayer of thanks, Lionel checked his watch. "We'd better eat and get going quickly. Even though we've had some down time, if we hurry we can still make it before midnight."

ॐ

As instructed, Lionel used his cell phone to call the factory when they were an hour away.

Unlike the rest of their trip, much of this portion was made in silence. Gwen hadn't said much since they left the truck stop, so neither had he. To fill the void of silence, he'd turned on the radio. The news reported minor structural damage to some homes and businesses, and as the man from one of the cars during their brief encounter with the tornado had said, there were only a few minor injuries, and that was it.

Apparently life was back to normal.

Except Lionel didn't know what normal was anymore.

He felt a certain satisfaction knowing they had done a good job as a team to deliver their payload as quickly and efficiently as possible, but that also meant their journey was over. He didn't want to think about what came next.

When they reached the city limits, he pulled out the paper with the directions he'd been given on the phone and directed Gwen through the outskirts of the city to the industrial area.

While they waited for a traffic light that was only a few blocks away from their destination, Gwen turned to him. "Are you sure you're not going to be embarrassed about this?"

Lionel blinked. "Embarrassed? What for? We've made great time."

She turned her head forward. "That you're a passenger and that a woman is driving."

The light turned green, so she started moving the truck forward.

He grinned. "Not as embarrassed as you're going to be."

"Me? I don't care about being seen driving a truck. That's what I planned to do all summer."

He raised his arms and linked his fingers behind his head as he leaned back in the seat. "I know. But in four minutes you're going to have to back the trailer into the loading bay."

"Uh. . .back up?"

"You know. Driving backwards. Going in reverse to maneuver the trailer through a teeny little tunnel-like path to the warehouse door so they can unload their machinery, while at an angle, judging from the age of this complex. And the only way to see what you're doing is by looking in the mirror. In the dark. And you have to match the trailer door to the warehouse door within inches. And get it straight."

"Uh oh. I'm not very good at backing up. When I first started this, I thought it would be so easy. I thought it would be just like backing the boat into the water when we go camping, or backing the tent-trailer into the campsite, but on a larger scale like this, it turned out to be not as easy as I thought."

"Most beginning drivers practice backing up a load at the truck stops where there's lots of room. I did when I first got my license."

"I haven't had that kind of time. I haven't practiced at all except for the minimum needed to pass my test."

"I also spent a little time doing a temporary stint doing yard shunt work, so I'm better at backing up than most long-haul drivers. I'm open to bribery. I'll back it in for you. For the right price."

When no answer was forthcoming, Lionel wondered if he should duck to avoid flying objects.

Fortunately for him, she slowed and stopped in front of a gate, where a security guard used a radio to announce their arrival, then pointed them in the direction of the shipping/receiving area.

Just like many industrial areas in the older sections of various cities, this was exactly what he'd expected. When the neighborhood was designed, the distance between the buildings and property lines and fences had considered only the five-ton trucks and smaller trailers. Previous to twenty years ago, most shipping areas had been designed for a maximum trailer length of forty-five feet, which was the longest standard trailer length at the time. Ten years ago the standard had changed to forty-eight foot trailers, and now the new standard size had become fifty-three feet, which was what they were pulling. In a tight area like this, those eight feet made a big difference, especially for a beginner.

He opened his mouth to volunteer to switch places and back it in for her, but she spoke first.

"Okay, I give. What's the right price for you to back it in? Quick, before they notice."

He opened his mouth to say the first thing that popped into his mind, but stopped himself in time. He had almost said that he would back the trailer in for her for a kiss. "I'll think of something later. Let's trade places."

Because of her height, he didn't have to adjust the seat, and they switched drivers in seconds flat. A man appeared at the driver's door, and Lionel rolled down window to talk to him. He calculated the distance to where the man was pointing, shifted into reverse, jackknifed the unit as he backed up to get around the corner, and backed in. They both hopped out, and he cranked down the landing legs while Gwen locked the trailer brakes and unhooked the air lines. When they got the signatures for delivering the load in good order and all was settled, he and Gwen hopped back into the truck and exited the compound. Again, Gwen was driving.

"We did it." He could hear the pride in her voice. It wasn't her first trip, because she'd already been out once with Chad, but this was her first doubles run, and it had been a dandy. It was his first-ever doubles run as well, one he would never forget.

"Yes, we did. We make a good team. I think we must have done it in record time."

"So, what now?"

Lionel flattened the map in his lap and pulled his flashlight out of the glove box. "Now we go to the terminal at Evansville and report in, turn in the paperwork, and book off until the next load."

Just the thought of booking off for a sleep made him yawn. "Sorry," he said, making no effort to cover his mouth. She'd probably seen him do far worse already, and he simply didn't have the energy left to be polite. He'd been driving for twelve days without any time off, and the last few weren't exactly a normal pace. He'd been getting less sleep than usual in the past few days, and the pattern they'd fallen into had him going down for the night around midnight. It was nearly one in the morning. "I figure it will take about an hour to get to the terminal building from where we are." He yawned again.

"Why don't you have a nap? I've got a good memory. I'm a teacher, remember. Read me the directions, and I'm sure I can find my own way there."

Lionel started to fight another yawn, but gave up; after all, there was no point. "I think I'll do that," he spoke through his yawn. "And don't be afraid to open the curtain on me. I'll just kick off my sneakers and lie down just like this for a short nap. Wake me up when we get there. See you in an hour."

At her nod, he went to the back, pulled down the bunk, crawled in, and pulled the lightest blanket over his shoulders. He couldn't remember his pillow being so soft, or the motion of the truck being so soothing.

He knew he was falling asleep with a smile on his face. They delivered their load in good time, Gwen was driving, and all was fine.

&

"Lionel? Lionel? Wake up."

Slowly he opened one eye, then the other one. Gwen's face above him slowly came into focus. "Are we there already?"

She smiled, and he smiled back. She was smiling at him. He closed his eyes again to help him remember this moment.

She grabbed his shoulder and started shaking him. "Wake up!"

His eyes sprang open, but he grabbed his pillow and rolled his face into it to filter out the light. "Five minutes. . ." he mumbled and closed his eyes again.

In the back of his mind, something wasn't connecting. Something was wrong, different than it should have been.

He sat up with a jolt and blinked repeatedly. It was daylight.

"Why did you let me sleep so long?" The entire truck shook at the same time as a thud sounded. "What's going on?" Instead of hearing trucks, he heard the grinding of what he thought might be conveyors and the clanking of machinery. "Where are we?"

"I think we should talk."

Since the curtain was wide open, he looked forward out the front window of the cab. Not only was it daylight, but they weren't at the truck terminal anymore.

Gwen's cheeks darkened. "We're going back to Kansas."

"Kansas? What are you talking about?"

"It kind of happened like this. You were sleeping so soundly I didn't have the heart to wake you, so I took the paperwork into the terminal myself. I asked about how I was getting home, now that this big rush is over. I thought maybe I could fly home, but they said they have another rush load, and their own drivers are already dispatched out, so he gave it to us. It's a short hop back to Kansas for a doubles team. And I thought about what you said about getting fired if you refused a load. I didn't want to take the chance that they could fire you because of me, so I accepted it. That's where we are now, we're at a roofing place. We're taking a load of shingles to repair a church roof. The owner of the business is donating them. Seems the pastor there is an old friend. He wants them delivered as soon as possible. So I left you to sleep and we're at the shingle place now. I didn't even do too bad a job of backing it up myself. They directed me to a big wide open loading area, so it didn't matter that it was a little crooked. I thought I'd wake you up and tell you what was happening before the noise and shaking woke you up."

"Let me get this straight. You accepted a load, drove there, and they're loading the trailer right now."

"Yes. And you won't believe what happened. While you were sleeping, for the first time I got to be part of a real convoy."

All he could do was blink and stare at her.

"It was so much fun! I always wondered how trucks could go in such tight formation like that. Uncle Chad and I traveled with other trucks, but this was the first time I've been with more than three at a time. But now I was part of a real convoy! And I was driving all by myself! I think there were ten trucks all together in the line. We chatted on the CB and everything."

"But—"

"Now I know how they do it. Courtesy, and signaling. I closed in on the truck ahead of me, signaled left, and then pulled out into the passing lane and sped up. There wouldn't have been room for the length of the truck in between any in line when I wanted to get back, but all I had to do was signal right, and the truck I wanted to get in front of just flashed his brights to let me know he's going to fall back, and he was ever-so-nice and let me in."

"When—"

"And I made sure to double click on my turn signal to say thanks because Uncle Chad said to always do that. I'm never going to feel the same when I get back home and I'm driving my car."

"I—"

"Some people are such selfish morons behind the wheel of a car, it would be so nice if everyone could drive like those truckers. I don't know why people have to be so aggressive and nasty and risk their lives to get ahead by fifteen seconds. But anyway, here we are, almost ready to go with our next priority load. Were you going to say something?"

Lionel buried his face in his palms. "I was going to book off for a day before I accepted another trip. I've been driving for twelve days, and I need a break."

"I know, but I didn't know what to do. I'm sorry."

He shook his head. "What time is it?"

"It's a little after seven in the morning. We're not far from the terminal, don't worry. If there's something I forgot, we can go back on our way to Kansas."

He raised his head and checked his watch. She was right. "I went to sleep at one. What have you been doing for six hours?"

"Don't forget, it took an hour to get to the terminal after you fell asleep. And we're about an hour away from the terminal now."

"That's two. What about the other four hours?"

"I went into the lunchroom."

"By yourself?"

"I wasn't alone. There were all the other drivers going in and out. Lots of them sat for a while and talked to me. The graveyard shift foreman sat with me for a while, and we talked, too. And, also, some of the warehousemen came in every once in a while to talk to me, but I don't think they were supposed to do that. Everyone was really nice. Although, I didn't get any time to read my book. I don't think it's ever taken me this long to finish a book in my life."

Lionel flopped down on his back and stared at the ceiling. First she'd participated in a convoy, and now she'd gone into a building full of truck drivers and night shift warehousemen, a gorgeous woman all by herself. Of course she hadn't had a minute alone.

"They bought me coffee and everything. Some of them even offered to share their lunches, since I couldn't get to the fridge because you were sleeping. They were all so nice."

"I'll bet they were."

"Since you're awake, you might as well come with me. There are a few men here who invited me to come into the lunchroom while I wait for them to finish loading the shingles. They're really nice, too. I told them my driving partner was sleeping in the truck. They suggested I leave you alone, but I thought it best to wake you up."

Lionel slapped his hands over his eyes and groaned. "You did the right thing. Let's go join them for coffee."

❧

They made good time on the road, although driving alongside the tourists in the daytime slowed them down to some degree. They finally reached their destination mid-afternoon, and

Gwen promised Lionel they would book off for a day, no matter what, so they could both catch up on some much-needed sleep. She could feel the effects of three short nights' sleep in a row herself, and knowing how tired he was after being away from home for so long made her almost feel guilty about accepting the load. But she had had to make a decision, and so she made it. She would have felt guiltier if he'd lost his job because of her.

Gwen read the directions to Lionel as he drove through the small town. They headed into an older district in the town's core, where the homes were smaller and, one thing Gwen would never have noticed before she started driving a truck, the roads were narrower.

"It should be just after the next left."

They approached a rectangular old church building. Dark green bushes dotted with red flowers stood on either side of the front doors. They appeared to be in better condition than the building. The white slatboard walls were peeling in sections, and the short steeple was peeling more than the rest of the building. It didn't have a cross on it, but the sides were open, indicating a bell inside. Gwen wondered if they actually rang the old bell on Sunday morning and what it would sound like. Orange tarps covered sections of the roof, and the parking lot was empty except for one small car and a huge blue disposal bin.

Lionel drove carefully into the parking lot, going slowly over the old cracked surface.

"What's your church like at home?" he asked.

Gwen looked at the tattered building. "It's nothing like this. The church I go to at home is huge, and the building is only about fifteen years old and very modern, inside and out. But I've always appreciated a classic old building, although this one is more classic than most."

They walked inside and found their way to the pastor's office. A man close to retirement age sat behind a very cluttered desk, talking on the phone. The room wasn't much bigger than the desk. He motioned them to a couple of chairs and they squeezed into the limited space while he ended his call.

"Welcome! I'm John Funk, the pastor at this humble place. What can I do for you?"

Lionel stood and returned the pastor's handshake. "We've got a load of shingles for you, Pastor Funk. They're from a friend of yours in Indiana."

John Funk pumped Lionel's hand faster. "Praise the Lord! The roof wasn't in very good shape as it was, but the wind and hail finished it off. Those shingles are an answer to prayer. And please, call me John."

Lionel nodded. "Pleased to meet you, Pastor John. I'm Lionel, and this is Gwen."

Gwen shook the man's hand in turn.

Pastor John checked his watch. "You're here much earlier than I ever hoped you would be, and I appreciate it. You must be hungry. Would the two of you like to be my guests for dinner?"

Gwen shook her head. "No, that's okay. I know my pastor at home is always having people over for dinner, and I don't know how his wife does it on short notice. But thanks for the offer."

Pastor John smiled warmly. "Your pastor at home? So you're a believer? Praise the Lord. About that dinner, I happen to know it's leftover turkey dinner, and there's lots."

Gwen opened her mouth to decline, but before she spoke, she turned to Lionel. At the mention of turkey dinner, his whole face lit up. She imagined he didn't get many home-cooked meals and, of those he did, probably very few were full turkey dinners, first day or leftovers.

She knew his answer without asking.

"Thank you, that would be lovely. We'd be delighted to join you for dinner. But only if it's no trouble for you or your wife."

"I'll phone and check, but I know what the answer will

be. I've been married to the same woman for thirty-seven years, and I'd like to think I know her reactions. Just don't tell her she's predictable."

The phone call yielded exactly the results he'd expected. While Pastor John locked up the church, Lionel locked up the truck, and within minutes they stopped in front of a small white slatboard house. Rather than fences, evergreen hedges separated the yards, the twisted old shrubbery denoting the age of the well-established and well-kept older neighborhood.

A gray-haired woman dressed in jeans and a bright green T-shirt waited in the doorway. "Welcome, Lionel and Gwen. I'm Freda. You don't know how much it means to have those shingles here so soon. John can get started on some of it tonight, and hopefully it will be done in a few days and we'll be ready for the next rain."

"A few days?" Gwen asked. "Why do you think it's going to take that long? It's not that big a building. You don't mean you're going to do it all by yourself?"

He shrugged his shoulders. "It's a small congregation. Today is Friday, so everyone is at work. They have their own messes to clean up and repairs to make on Saturday. And I won't ask anyone to work on the church roof on Sunday. I doubt most of them are aware of the extent of the damage to the old roof. But it will get done."

Gwen looked at Lionel, and Lionel looked at her. They both raised their eyebrows and nodded at the same time.

Lionel turned back to Pastor John. "We've got a day here before we have to take another load out. If you've got a couple of extra hammers, we can help with the roof, and it will be done before Sunday morning."

"I can't ask you to do that. You're not even a member of our congregation."

Lionel glanced at Gwen and smiled. Her heart swelled with pride for him as he spoke.

"We're all members of God's congregation, no matter where

in the world we live. If you've got hammers, you've got help."

Gwen nodded. She didn't want to be a burden, and she certainly didn't want to sit and do nothing while Lionel worked during the short amount of time they had off. "And I'm not too bad with a hammer, either," she said.

The Funks joined hands. "I don't know what to say. . ." Pastor John drawled.

Lionel grinned from ear to ear and patted his stomach. "Just say it's supper time!"

Gwen elbowed him in the ribs. "*That* was delicate," she muttered under her breath so only Lionel could hear.

He laughed and followed the Funks into the house.

After a prayer of thanks for the food, the gift of the shingles, and the unexpected help to install them, they enjoyed the wonderful meal Freda set before them. Not that the truck stop food had been bad, but it hadn't taken long for Gwen to become tired of greasy fare, which made her consider the leftovers an extra special treat. Lionel ate with utter abandon, devouring everything on his plate as if it were a king's meal placed before a starving man.

She nudged his ankle under the table. She had meant just to get his attention, but at the contact he froze, fork in midair, and stared at her. "Yes?" he asked.

"Nothing," Gwen mumbled.

He obviously didn't get the hint, because when Freda passed him more food, he gratefully accepted it.

Freda offered more to Gwen, but she shook her head. "This has been wonderful, but I've eaten so much. Thank you, I couldn't eat another bite."

"But I have homemade cherry pie for dessert."

Gwen really was full, but she couldn't refuse the kind woman. "Well, just a small piece, that would be lovely. Thank you."

Lionel's eyes lit up. "Homemade pie?"

Gwen couldn't stand it anymore. When Pastor John rose to clear the table and Freda went to the counter to cut the pie, Gwen turned and whispered to Lionel. "I can't believe you. You look like you haven't seen food for a week. Aren't you embarrassed?"

"Me? You should talk. You're the one with the hollow leg. I eat like this once and you think it's a big deal, but you're the one who orders a second helping of fries at six in the morning."

She was about to comment on the unique seasoning of the fries in question, when Freda returned and placed two plates of pie, topped with ice cream, in front of them. "So, where are you folks from?"

"We're from Vancouver, Canada."

"You're a long way from home."

"Yes, we are."

"I hear it rains a lot there."

Gwen smiled. "It rains a lot, but it's not as much as people think it does. I really don't mind the rain."

Lionel harumphed beside her as he dug into the delicious homemade pie. "I hate the rain."

Gwen took a nibble of her pie. "You were the one praying for rain just before we ran into the hail."

"I never did."

"You did so. You said that you wanted a little rain to break the heat."

One eyebrow quirked. "I might have said that, but I certainly never prayed for it. You like rain so much, you probably prayed for it, you just won't admit it."

The sparkle in his eye gave his thoughts away. Even though she knew he was teasing and goading her to put her foot in her mouth, she was having too much fun to stop. Gwen opened her mouth to tell him that the reason they were caught in the storm was his fault, when she heard the older couple snickering. She snapped her mouth shut and lowered her head to pick at the piece of pie in front of her.

Freda smiled and snickered. "Don't mind us. As pastor and wife, we've seen a lot of marriages over the course of the years, and more couples would benefit from this kind of friendly banter. How long have you two been married?"

Gwen felt her face heat up. She glanced at Lionel out of the corner of her eye, noting that he was also blushing.

Gwen delicately dabbed her mouth with her napkin. "We're not married."

Freda's cheeks reddened as well. "I just assumed. . .You're traveling together. . ."

Lionel laid his cutlery down on his plate. "Gwen started driving with her uncle, but an emergency breakdown teamed us together on short notice. And since we're driving team, the company sent us on another priority trip, which was your shingles. We actually just met at the beginning of the summer."

Freda's hands rose to her cheeks. "Oh!"

"Yes. I must say it was a surprise to both of us, but God was gracious to team us together as Christians. To tell the truth, this is the first time since we've been traveling together that we have some time off and don't have to drive all night. I was wondering if you could recommend a motel nearby."

Both of them stared at Lionel as he spoke. Gwen chose to keep silent. She knew what they were thinking.

Lionel's ears flamed. "The motel room is for Gwen. I'll be sleeping in the truck."

Freda turned to Gwen. "Nonsense. You don't have to get a motel. Please, be our guest in our home for the night. There's just the two of us here, we have a spare bedroom. You're more than welcome." She stopped to smile, making Gwen think of how much of an art it was for the woman to recover her composure so quickly. "You'd be welcome even if you weren't helping fix the roof of the church."

Gwen noticed she didn't offer for Lionel to also be a guest in their home, nor had Freda suggested that she take her to the motel after all and that Lionel stay in their guest room so he wouldn't have to sleep in the truck.

She tried to think of a way to politely decline in favor of the motel, when Pastor John spoke.

"If you sleep here instead of across town at the motel, we'll get an earlier start on the roof."

Gwen smiled. "That would be lovely. Thank you. Now let me help with the dishes."

nine

Lionel sat outside the church and waited for everyone to arrive. The sun was up and he was refreshed and ready.

He couldn't believe it when Pastor John had left him with the key to the church so he could have washroom facilities if he needed them. The old building didn't have a kitchen or a shower, but it had the basics, and that was all he needed. In his travels as a trucker, it was more than he had most trips.

What astounded him the most was the trust involved in giving him the key. They had just met the night before, and nothing would have stopped him from loading up anything of value from inside the church and leaving in the middle of the night. Of course, they had Gwen at their home, and he wasn't going anywhere without her.

He'd phoned the nearest terminal to book off the day, and they had told him he would have had the weekend off anyway, since there wasn't a load out, which was fine with Lionel.

It gave him extra time with Gwen, which was exactly what he wanted since they would now be on their way home and their time together would soon be over. Not that being up on the roof and banging away at shingles was exactly quality time, but it was as close as he would get. It was quieter and more private in the truck when they were driving, but that was work, and with the work came limitations and boundaries.

He looked up at the roof. Whatever he said and did today with Gwen would be on display to not only a minister but the entire neighborhood. He looked up to the clear blue sky. God was always watching, day or night, in public or in the privacy of his home and his truck. Rather than being intimidating, the knowledge gave him great comfort. Today he didn't have to think about calculating maximum driving hours or crossing any personal lines while in the confines of his truck. He could concentrate everything he had on Gwen, and he prayed that God would bless their short time together away from business.

Pastor John's small car pulled into the parking lot, and Pastor John, Freda, and Gwen climbed out.

"Good morning, son. Did you sleep well?"

"Yes, sir, I did."

He had slept well. After dinner they'd cleaned up and talked and prayed together before Pastor John dropped him off for the night. On the short drive back to the church, Lionel had been under the impression that Pastor John was on the verge of asking him about his relationship with Gwen, but at the last minute held back, which was a good thing. Lionel didn't know the answer.

After their experience with the edge of the tornado, he'd thought briefly that he could have been in love with her but recognized that the panic of the situation had intensified his emotions. Of course he liked her, and he liked her a lot, but it couldn't be love, not after such a short amount of time. However, whatever was happening between them had hit him hard and fast. When they parted ways, Gwen would be taking a piece of him with her. He vowed that, today, he would do all he could to discover more about this fast friendship and make the most of it, although what he felt for her at this point extended beyond anything he'd ever felt in his heart for any friend, male or female.

"I haven't re-shingled a roof in years, but I remember how it's done and all the steps. I want to tell you again how much I appreciate this. Freda won't be coming up on the roof, she'll be inside the church doing some paperwork, and she's brought drinks and meals. And we brought something for breakfast for you, since we all ate at home."

Lionel wiped his hands on his pants and accepted an English muffin with bacon and eggs inside. "This is great.

Thanks." He gobbled it down while Gwen and Pastor John set the ladder against the eaves.

Gwen returned with something in her hand. He expected her to hand him a napkin, but instead it was a small white bottle. "Put this on. It's sunscreen."

"Sunscreen? What do I need this for?"

"For your right arm, but do both."

"I beg your pardon?"

She grabbed both his wrists and pulled his arms forward and together. Her touch caught him so off guard that he nearly dropped the bottle.

"See? Look at the difference. Your left arm is nice and tanned, and your right arm is white."

"So? That happens all the time. It's from driving with my arm out the window."

"Exactly my point. Don't you think you'll look stupid with one normal arm and one beet red arm if you don't put on lots of sunscreen?"

He wanted to protest, but for such a minor point, despite how silly, he didn't want to look stupid in front of Gwen. It shouldn't have mattered, but it did.

Lionel splashed on the sunscreen and rubbed it into his arms and face. "This stuff stinks. I'm only doing this for you, you know."

She harumphed and turned her back to him, but he caught her sticking her tongue out at him first. "Spare me. Such a sacrifice. How will I ever live with myself?"

"You can make it up to me later."

She made a sound almost like a snort, which surprised him. He didn't know what to say, so he said nothing.

Once everyone was sufficiently coated with sunscreen, Freda held the ladder and they climbed up to the roof. The first chore was to pull off the old shingles and tarpaper and toss everything into the disposal bins below. He'd discovered one bin on each side of the building, and he imagined they would overflow them both by the time they were done.

The old shingles were brittle and often cracked. He cleared one section, then moved to start in another place when a hunk of shingles and tarpaper flew over the peak toward him. It fell apart mid-flight, with a large section falling near his feet and sliding down the roof and into the bin. A smaller section of broken shingle sailed over his head, and another small section hit his back.

"Hey!" he called out. "Watch it!"

A scuffle sounded on the other side, and Gwen appeared from the other side of the peak. "Oh, Lionel! I'm so sorry! Are you okay?"

He forced himself to grimace. "No, I'm mortally wounded." He slapped both palms over his heart. "I need first aid. Artificial respiration would help."

Another small piece of shingle hit him in the stomach. "In your dreams," she muttered, and disappeared on the other side of the roof once more.

He couldn't help but smile as he bent to pull off another section. It would have been nice, but what he pictured in his mind was more personal than artificial respiration. It hadn't been long since they'd met, but he caught himself calculating the days until they were back at the home terminal. At first he hadn't wanted to drive with her, and now he wasn't ready for their time together to be over.

It had bothered him more than he cared to admit when she had said she was considering flying home. He didn't know she'd been uncomfortable with him, even though the situation they found themselves in, especially as Christians, was admittedly difficult.

Lionel froze, then stared at the torn tarpaper in his hand without really seeing it. He had just realized he wanted more than a driving partnership with Gwen. He wanted a real relationship, both business and personal, something that would last. And today was probably going to be the only day he could use to build their relationship into something more than it was. Once they were driving again, he couldn't say or do anything that would make her feel compromised or ill at ease when they couldn't get away from each other in the close confines of the truck.

When summer was over and she was back to her life as a teacher, Lionel wanted to be able to call her up when he was in town and spend as much time with her as she would allow. And when they were apart, he would have his computer. He could always practice to improve his typing and send her E-mail messages, although he didn't want merely a long-distance relationship. He needed the real thing.

"Coffee time!" Freda called out from below.

Lionel wiped the damp hair off his forehead and rested his hands on his hips as he surveyed what they'd done so far. Only one section remained to strip, then they would begin stapling on the tarpaper. After that, they'd have to get the bundles of shingles lifted up onto the roof and start nailing them down. He had no idea how long such an area would take.

Gwen climbed up over the peak and stood beside him. "It didn't look so large from the ground, did it?"

"No. I'm glad we started at sunrise."

"Yes, it's already starting to get hot."

The stubborn lock of hair fell into his face again, and he swiped it away. "I don't think it ever cools down in this part of the country."

"That's what I've heard, too."

He steadied the ladder at the top while she climbed down, and they joined Pastor John and Freda in the shade. When Gwen went inside to wash up, he added the milk and sugar to her coffee, then sat on the grass and stretched out his legs, waiting for her to return.

The pastor and his wife discussed some church business between themselves, which was fine with Lionel, because he didn't feel like talking anyway. He lay down on his back on the cool grass, linked his fingers behind his head, and looked up at the clear blue sky, waiting for Gwen's return.

While he waited, he anticipated her pretty smile as she took that first sip of the coffee he'd poured for her, just the way she liked it. She truly appreciated the little things he did for her, which made him want to do more.

He quickly nixed the idea of doing her laundry. She'd made it more than clear she didn't want him looking at her stuff. Of course, he didn't exactly like the idea of her handling his underwear either, even if it was out of the necessity of doing laundry. He tried to think of something else.

Another thing she would appreciate was for him to play her favorite music in the boring moments on the road. Not that there were many boring moments. They seemed to fill almost every minute with conversation of some sort. Even when they weren't laughing about something stupid one of them had done, their serious moments were equally as pleasant. They'd been open and honest with each other, talking about things he'd never spoken to anyone about, even his best friend. Yet, for everything they discussed, no matter how personal, they both had been able to tell before they'd reached the point of prying into an area best left alone. Every time they'd prayed together had been special, too.

Not moving from his stretched out position on the ground, Lionel closed his eyes and smiled at his own thoughts. He'd caught himself plotting to impress a woman, something he'd never done, not even with Sharon, the woman he'd asked to marry him. At the time he hadn't seen it, but he could now, in hindsight, see where Sharon had worked to impress him without his knowing it, and it had worked. She'd done all the right things to feed his ego, and after living with the dysfunctional relationship between his parents, he hadn't seen it coming. He'd been too starved for her attention to realize she'd been stringing him along. Instead of missing him when he was out driving, his absence had been convenient for her.

Gwen was different fom anyone he'd ever known. She'd done nothing to impress him, and instead of trying to feed his ego to make him putty in her hands, as Sharon had done so well, Gwen pointed out his flaws and liked him anyway. She laughed with him, understood his weaknesses, and accepted him exactly as he was. Likewise, she took it in stride when he teased her. Even when they were working, they had fun together.

"Lionel? Are you sleeping?"

If he was, he would have been dreaming about her. He opened one eye. "Just relaxing."

"I see you poured my coffee. Thank you." He watched as she took a long slow sip, cradling the mug in her hands and smiling, just like he knew she would.

He opened the other eye. "So, do I get a tip?"

Her eyes sparkled, her mouth opened, and he anticipated a smart comeback, but instead she glanced at the Funks, who were not necessarily paying attention but would clearly hear anything she said.

"Put it on my tab," she said, winked, and took a second sip.

As soon as they were finished drinking their coffee, the three of them returned to the roof and tore off the last of the old shingles. Soon they had the new tarpaper laid out and stapled down, and next came the job of moving the new bundles of shingles from the truck to the roof.

Using a winch and a few lengths of rope attached to the steeple, Pastor John rigged up a way to raise the bundles of shingles to the roof. They worked quickly as the dwindling coolness of the morning gave way to the full heat of a summer day. Gwen pushed the bundles out of the trailer, Pastor John worked the winch, and Lionel insisted on being the one to distribute the bundles on the surface of the roof. As he carried each new bundle farther and placed them down where they would be needed, he could feel the effects of the unaccustomed physical labor. Every bundle seemed to become heavier than the bundle before it. By the time he heaved the last one into place on the far side of the roof, he was dripping with sweat. He ached all over. He couldn't see people doing this for a living. He much preferred sitting in his air-conditioned truck.

With every kink in his back and twinge in his arms, he

reminded himself that this was work for the Lord.

He sat on the peak to rest, not having the energy to climb down the ladder for a glass of water. Gratefully he accepted one that Gwen brought up to him. He drank most of it, then, when no one was looking, he dumped the last bit of it over his head and wiped the soothing cool water down his face and over the back of his neck.

The work of nailing down the shingles wasn't as bad as carrying them, but the heat of the noonday sun made it more difficult to endure and finally forced them to stop.

Freda filled four glasses from a pitcher, then picked up two glasses, kept one, and gave one to Pastor John. Gwen also picked up two glasses and handed one to Lionel, standing very close as he took it from her hand.

She leaned toward his ear. "Don't pour this one over your head, okay?" she whispered. "It's lemonade, and this time it would be sticky."

He opened his mouth to protest, but he couldn't think of a thing to say.

Gwen pushed her damp hair off her face and smiled at him. Temporarily, he felt better. "Actually, it was a good idea, and I did the same thing after you did. Only no one saw me."

"I'm not used to this heat. It's really wiping me out."

"The heat doesn't help, but you're the one who insisted on carrying all the shingles yourself. Are you crazy?"

"I couldn't let an older man carry those heavy bundles up there in the heat. I'm in the prime of life, you know." He made a fist and pressed it into the center of his chest. As he spoke, he could feel the wetness from his shirt seep between his fingers. The gel in his hair had given up its hold long ago and his damp hair hung into his face. He didn't care enough to push it back.

In order to protect his knees when he knelt on the shingles, he'd worn jeans instead of shorts. The denim was also wet with sweat and stuck to his legs. His feet ached, made worse because granules from the shingles had worked their way inside his sneakers. He didn't want to take his sneakers off, fearing that once they came off he'd never get them back on. He hit himself in the chest a few times and grunted like an ape. *And why not?* he thought, because by now he probably smelled like an ape.

One corner of Gwen's mouth tilted up as she scanned him from head to toe. "Prime of life, huh? You look it."

Lionel looked at Gwen. Even damp from the heat and showing the signs of heavy work, she still looked good.

"Come on," he said, tilting his head toward the Funks. "Let's eat."

While Freda opened the cooler, he went inside the church to wash up and splash some cold water on his face.

He longed for the air-conditioning in his truck but settled for the quasi cool of the shade in the churchyard. While they ate, Pastor John shared many funny stories of his experiences over the years. Lionel looked forward to hearing his sermon Sunday morning. Being able to attend a service inside a real church was a rare treat for Lionel, since he spent most weekends on the road.

Too soon they were back at work, nailing down the shingles. He didn't know why he thought he would be able to talk to Gwen while they were working, because she was spending all of her time on one side of the roof helping Pastor John, and he was working alone on the other side of the building.

"Supper time!" Freda called from below.

Lionel dropped the hammer without a second's hesitation. He was the first to wash up and be ready.

In the middle of their prayers before the meal, Freda's cell phone rang. She excused herself to answer it, and when she returned, her face was pale. Pastor John excused himself while the two of them talked in private, then returned.

"A crisis has come up with one of the members of the congregation. One of our youth is in the hospital from what appears to be a gang-related incident, although he appears to have been an innocent bystander, not directly involved. I'm going to join the family in the hospital, and that means I'm not going to be able to do any more work on the roof today. I don't expect to be back before nightfall."

Gwen gasped and raised her hands to her mouth. "You mean there are gangs here? In a small town like this?"

"There are gangs everywhere, unfortunately. Although he was in the city when this happened. I hate to stop now, but this is critical."

Lionel checked his watch. "We've still got lots of time. Leave us here and you go see to that family."

Freda glanced between them, shuffling her feet.

Lionel smiled at her, knowing what she was thinking. "Don't worry about us, Freda. If you feel you should go, then go. We'll be fine."

The Funks glanced quickly between each other. Freda reached into her pocket and picked a key off her key ring. "You've already got the church key. Here's our house key. Help yourself to anything in our home, with our gratitude. We appreciate all you've done for us. I don't know when we'll be back." She grasped his hand, then Gwen's. "Thank you."

"You're welcome," Lionel and Gwen mumbled in unison.

Without further word, the Funks hurried to the car and drove off.

Lionel rested one fist on his hip as he swiped a damp lock of hair off his forehead and gazed upward to the half-finished roof. "Do you think we stand much chance of getting it finished before nightfall? How much is done on the other side?"

"More than on this side, but there's still lots to do."

He sent Gwen up the ladder while he steadied it, then climbed up himself and got back to work.

Earlier he had worked alone in silence, but he'd heard Gwen and Pastor John talking as they worked. Even if he couldn't hear the words they'd been speaking, he'd heard the sound of happy conversation. Now all he heard was the hammering and the resulting echo in the distance. It wasn't nearly as comforting.

By the time they reached the peak, Lionel estimated under an hour until the sun would set. They worked quickly, with Gwen curving the shingles over the peak and holding them in place as Lionel hammered them down as fast as he could. Now that they were finally close enough to talk, he didn't. It would have taken too much energy to speak and hammer at the same time. Stubbornness alone kept him going, boosted by the challenge to beat the sun before it disappeared.

"We did it!" Gwen half cheered and half groaned as he hammered in the last nail.

Lionel laid the hammer down. He'd never worked so hard in his life. He was so thirsty his throat felt like sandpaper, and his sweat-soaked T-shirt stuck to his chest in a most uncomfortable way. All he had the energy to do was groan as he let himself sink down, half-lying and half-sitting on the roof. He leaned his back against the slope of the roof, resting his elbows behind him on the peak, and bent his knees to use his heels to brace himself from sliding down.

"The sun will be down in a few minutes."

"Yeah," he mumbled. He wanted to pull the wet T-shirt away from his skin, but he didn't want to do something so disgusting in front of Gwen. Besides, he didn't think he could move.

To his shock, she sat down beside him. He wanted to shift away, but he was too tired. If he had to get up, he wouldn't sit down again, he would go all the way and get off the roof. Fortunately, he was downwind. They sat in silence and watched the sky turn colors as the sun set.

"Isn't the sky beautiful?" Gwen asked with a wistful sigh. "Is it really true that if the sky is all pink and purple, it will be good weather the next day?"

"Sometimes, but I'm always moving, so I don't stay with the local weather system for long."

"It's finally cooling down a little."

He didn't think so. He figured the temperature still hadn't dipped below ninety, and even though he was covered in sweat, he was still too warm. He wasn't used to the heat, and he didn't like it. That's why he had air-conditioning in his truck. He could barely stand himself; he didn't know how Gwen could sit so close to him. He also wondered why women didn't sweat like men.

Gwen sighed again. "Old towns like this have always fascinated me. I wonder if some of the buildings nearby are heritage buildings?"

"I dunno," he muttered, trying to shuffle over with the least amount of effort.

She pointed north. "I think that area with that lit-up cement square in the middle and the flag is the town core. I'll bet the dark building is made of brick, and it's the police station. And that one with the flag in front would be city hall. What do you think?"

All he could think of was the need for a cold drink and a clean shirt. "Probably."

"You know those old black and white movies, where at the end the people sit on the flat rooftop of some old apartment block, looking out over the city? We're kind of doing the same thing. Isn't that fascinating?"

He thought that women were supposed to find that kind of thing romantic, not fascinating, but romance was the last thing he felt. He was sweaty, tired, thirsty, and he didn't feel like talking. What he wanted was a long shower, then a bed. "I guess. I don't watch old movies."

Gwen stretched. "We should get down before it's totally pitch-black. I guess the only way we're going to get back to the Funks' house is in the truck. I hope their neighbors don't mind."

At this point, Lionel didn't care who minded. With every movement, his muscles protested as he slowly made his way down the ladder and then steadied it while Gwen climbed down.

As they approached the truck, which he had parked on the farthest corner of the small parking lot after they had all the shingles out, he nearly groaned aloud. He knew they'd be using the truck to get back to the house, but what he hadn't considered was that it was still hooked to the trailer, and he couldn't take the set through the residential neighborhood.

"Oh dear," Gwen mumbled. "We've got to unhook before we can go."

If it wasn't so far, he would have considered walking. He really didn't want to go through all the work of unhooking, but he didn't have a choice. He stood in one spot, staring at the truck and trailer, trying to motivate himself to move.

He felt Gwen's light touch on his forearm. He gritted his teeth, forcing himself not to cringe away from her touch, but he really didn't want her touching him when he was like this.

"Lionel? Is something wrong?"

He shook his head to get himself moving. "I'm just thinking about unhooking so we can get going." He arched and twisted his sore back and began to unlatch the handle for the dolly legs.

Gwen didn't move. "I know how you feel. I'm so tired. I don't know if I can lift my arms."

It gave him little satisfaction to know he wasn't the only one feeling the after-effects of the physical labor from sunrise to sunset, literally. He gritted his teeth and cranked down the dolly legs, and Gwen unhooked the air lines and set the back trailer brakes.

Once they arrived at the house, Gwen let him shower first, and he was soon back in the truck. It was all he could do to drive back to the church parking lot. He couldn't remember ever being so tired. The second his head hit the pillow, he was out like a light.

ten

Gwen yawned as they drove into the church parking lot. She had no idea pastors got up so early on Sunday. She vividly remembered watching the sunset not all that long ago, and now, barely after sunrise, she was back at the church again.

Pastor John tried the front door of the church, but it was locked solid. A knock received no reply, and a check inside the windows showed that all inside was dark. Gwen walked across the parking lot to Lionel's truck, which was also dark and quiet inside.

She rapped lightly on the door. "Lionel? It's me. Are you sleeping?"

Nothing happened.

She knocked a little louder. "Lionel? Can you hear me?"

Still nothing moved. She stepped up onto the running board and peeked in the window. The curtain was drawn across the bunk area, and all was still.

Gwen knocked louder. "Lionel! Wake up! We need the church key!"

Finally the curtain moved. Gwen hopped down and waited beside the door until it opened.

Lionel leaned over the seat, one hand resting on the steering wheel, the other straight and supporting his weight as he leaned on the seat. His hair hung in his face, his eyes barely squinted open, and she'd never seen a more sour expression. "What time is it?" he mumbled.

"It's six-forty-two A.M."

"What are you doing here?"

"Pastor John wants to get ready for the Sunday service, and he needs the key for the church."

He grumbled something under his breath and backed up

very slowly. As he bent to retrieve the keys from the compartment in the dash, he flinched and pressed his left fist into the small of his back as he slowly straightened.

"Lionel? Are you okay?"

"I'm fine. Here's the key." Instead of bending over and handing to her, he tossed it from where he stood.

Gwen felt a little stiff herself after all that hard work yesterday, and knowing Lionel did most of the heavy lifting and all of the moving of the bundles of shingles once they'd gotten them moved to the roof, it didn't take a rocket scientist to know what was wrong. She also knew where he stowed his clothing and overnight bag for his first trip out of the truck when waking up, and he'd have to bend and stretch to get at it.

"Do you want some help?"

"No. Just let me wake up a bit."

"Okay. See you in a few minutes." Not that she thought he'd be any better once he switched his brain into gear.

She pushed the door closed to save him the agony of reaching for it. Before she took her first step, she heard him groan from inside the cab. She hurt inside knowing he was suffering, but she wouldn't invade his privacy to get his overnight bag for him.

Pastor John opened the door, punched in the alarm code, and continued inside. Gwen stood inside the doorway, watching the truck and waiting.

The passenger door opened and Lionel emerged, very slowly. He held himself poker-straight as he walked, without his usual speed or bounce, first trip of the morning or otherwise.

She held the door open for him as he entered. She noticed he was wearing the same clothes as when he left Pastor John's house the evening before, and he was very wrinkled.

"Are you sure you're okay?"

He didn't speak. But if looks could kill, she would have been six feet under.

She stayed in the foyer, not wanting to make it too obvious she was waiting for him. When he finally made his appearance, she followed him back outside. "Freda stayed home, and I'm supposed to drive you back because she's making you breakfast. It should be ready any minute. Are you ready to go?"

He opened his mouth like he was going to protest, and then his face sagged and his eyes closed while he spoke. "That would be great. I can't believe how stiff I am. I've got muscles that hurt where I didn't know I had muscles. This is so embarrassing."

They walked together to the car. "Don't be embarrassed. That was hard work, and for a lot of years you've had a job where you sit all day."

He winced as he used the roof of the car to support himself as he lowered his aching body into the car. "Rub it in, why don't you?"

She grinned. "Today you can pamper yourself. Freda's making you a wonderful bacon and egg breakfast, just the way you like it, and then we can relax and enjoy the service. After the services, she's invited us back as their guests for lunch. I thought it would be nice to go for an afternoon walk, which isn't a bad idea, because then you won't seize up completely. Then, after supper, we can go to the evening service. When was the last time you've been to church twice in one day?"

"Never."

"See? Today will be a real treat for you."

"Right."

"They're so grateful for the roof, it's almost embarrassing. They've invited us to stay with them tonight, too, but I don't want to impose on their hospitality."

"Me neither. But our only other choice is to have you hole up in a motel because we won't have a load out until Monday evening, and then only after we take the empty trailer back to the terminal in Topeka."

Gwen parked the car in front of the house. "Oh, and one

more thing. About the service. I didn't bring anything to wear except jeans and casual tops. What about you?"

"Same."

She frowned. "I hope we don't stick out too badly. I have no idea what everyone will be wearing, although the building itself is less than formal."

"I've never thought about what to wear. I've only ever worn jeans to church."

She stared at him. "Really?"

"Well, I've got this pair of khaki pants, but they're not much different than jeans, they're just a different color. But I didn't bring them, they're still at home."

Gwen remembered the family routine of going to church on Sunday as she grew up. As a girl, her mother made her wear pretty dresses to church, which annoyed her because she wasn't allowed to run outside and play with the boys when the service was over. As a teen she'd gone through a rebellious stage where she'd worn only jeans and T-shirts to the service, but it hadn't taken long to grow out of that stage of her life. Looking back, she realized her parents had it easy if that was the worst thing she'd done in her growing up years. Now, as an adult, she usually wore the same comfortable but suitably nice outfits she wore to school.

She thanked God for her Christian parents and her loving family, including her extended family, her Uncle Chad and Aunt Chelsea and her cousins.

"You told me you became a Christian as an adult. Does that mean your family never went to church when you were growing up? Not ever?"

His face hardened. "The only time my parents went near a church was for a wedding or a funeral."

She didn't think his brusque tone was exactly sarcasm, but if he didn't want to talk about it, she wouldn't press it.

They knocked on the door, and Freda enthusiastically welcomed them back. While they ate, Gwen joked about it being a rare treat to have two breakfasts in one day. Then she excused herself to dress for the service.

The three of them arrived back at the church as the worship team was beginning to practice the songs for the morning.

"We're sorry for making you so late in getting back," Lionel said as he held the door open for Gwen and Freda.

Freda smiled. "I always get here at this time. I usually drive John early and go back home so he can pray in private before the service and make sure everything is okay in the building. The worship team gets here about eight o'clock, and I come back about eight thirty to set up the table at the door and hand out bulletins until the ushers get here. I'll introduce you to the few people who also come early, and then leave you alone."

Gwen smiled at Lionel. If she wasn't mistaken, he looked nervous. She grew up going to church, but she suspected he felt out of place at an organized service where he didn't know anyone. A piece of her heart went out to him. She touched his hand, slipped her fingers between his, and held on. "Come on. Let's go get introduced, and then we'll visit with people until the service."

૨૦

Lionel smiled as Freda introduced them to one of the church's elder couples. The couple welcomed them and asked what he thought were the usual questions when greeting a newcomer, but he only half paid attention.

Gwen was holding his hand. He suspected she could sense his nervousness and was trying to make him feel better, but whatever the reason, Lionel determined to make the most of it. For today, the people here would perceive them not as a driving team, but as a couple, and that was exactly the way he intended to behave.

He closed his hand around Gwen's and gave her fingers a little squeeze. In response, she turned toward him and smiled. A smile meant just for him. He listened politely as she chatted with the growing group of people who surrounded them. Word seemed to spread that they were from out of town, because soon they were joined by another couple who started asking questions about vacation spots on the West Coast. Lionel had to confess he didn't know much about vacation spots. He traveled for a living but never stayed long enough at any one spot to enjoy it, and living out of a truck wasn't exactly vacation paradise. When it was time for his holidays, he tended to stay home and catch up on everything with his friends.

He listened to Gwen tell tales of her favorite vacation activity, which was camping. He recalled her saying something about her brother being a forest ranger, so he supposed that a love for the great outdoors was something that went in the family. He thought that for someone who seemed to thrive in a crowd, camping seemed a rather solitary activity.

More people entered, and many approached to chat. Lionel liked the friendly atmosphere prevalent throughout the whole place.

The demographics of the area were exactly what he expected, taking in mind the condition of the old building and the fact that they couldn't fix the church's roof if it weren't for the shingles being a donation. It was an older, slightly run-down area of town where housing was cheaper. The majority of the congregation was made up of either lower-income families or the elderly living on a fixed income. A few of the families in attendance appeared to have recently come out of a biker lifestyle. He guessed there were about 150 people in attendance, including the children, yet with the diversity in backgrounds, everyone here treated each other as equals and as Christian family.

When the worship time started, he was pleased to know a couple of the songs, and Gwen knew most of them, although none were in a style they were used to. He was used to a single guitar or taped music, and Gwen was used to a very polished and practiced worship team. This group of people was somewhere in the middle. What they lacked in skills perfected by lessons they more than made up for in eagerness and unpolished natural talent.

Unfortunately, he had to let go of Gwen's hand, because the congregation clapped to a couple of songs, something he wasn't used to, but Gwen joined in with enthusiasm. Gwen also raised her hands with a number of people in the congregation and prayed openly, while Lionel kept his hands at his sides or joined in front of himself and remained quiet. Knowing her passion for Jesus in her life outside church, her behavior inside wasn't surprising. He liked it.

As soon as they sat for the pastor's sermon, Gwen pulled out of her purse the smallest full-version Bible he'd ever seen. As soon as they were finished with the scripture reading, he again sought her hand. Her reaction indicated she hadn't expected it, but she didn't pull away.

He thoroughly enjoyed the pastor's sermon, and the service ended with a solemn and meaningful hymn.

"You said we were invited to Pastor John and Freda's for lunch after the service?"

Gwen nodded. "Yes. I think they're going to invite someone else, and we also have to wait until everyone is gone so he can lock up the building."

Lionel looked around the room. He'd always gone alone to church services, whether it was at home or on the road. This time, sitting beside Gwen, the room filled with families and people of all ages, was different than anything he'd ever done. It felt good. It felt right.

When they stood to talk with another couple who asked about their travels, he didn't drop her hand. Since life on the road was new to Gwen, he let her answer all the questions, since driving had become mundane for him years ago.

She was open and honest with everyone she spoke to, whether it was a child or an adult, and she spoke as an equal to all. He could see why she loved being a teacher. She was good at it. Everyone paid rapt attention to her, as did he. They never had a moment alone until the church doors were locked, and even then they talked in the parking lot with more people before they finally managed to get away.

All through lunch and the rest of the day, he participated little in any of the many conversations. He usually didn't feel comfortable in a crowd, but being with Gwen was different. Whether it was a small private group or the entire church congregation, he had Gwen at his side, and things that used to bother him were no longer important. Any time he was hesitant about saying anything or felt the push of too many people around him, she seemed to sense his hesitation and jumped into whatever topic was current until he could regain his bearings.

The times she got carried away with a subject, he could quietly interject and show her without words that it was time to settle down.

They were two halves of a whole.

If he was unsure before, he was sure now. He was deeply and fully in love with Gwen Lamont, his temporary driving partner.

eleven

"Good-bye, you two! And thanks again for everything!"

Gwen waved at Pastor John and Freda as they drove out of the church parking lot, beginning the trip back to Topeka and, ultimately, home.

She turned to Lionel. "They were such a nice couple. I'll have to write to them when I get home."

Lionel patted his pocket. "Yes, and I can't believe all the food they gave us. I got their E-mail address. I can't remember the last time I actually wrote a letter to someone. I don't like typing, but I like writing even less. Guess it's a guy thing."

"Or a *lazy* thing. Or maybe you're just too cheap to buy a stamp."

"You wound me."

Gwen didn't answer. She doubted anything she said could wound him, although she was starting to feel a wound opening in her own heart.

They were on their way home. Lionel had a program in his computer that was designed for truckers. It calculated that it would take them only thirty-two hours to get home. She wasn't sure she was ready to get home. The last week had been one unlike anything she'd ever experienced.

For all they'd been through and all they'd done, the week had gone fast, yet in other ways, it seemed like forever.

"I figure we'll be in Topeka in a couple of hours, and then we're going home, and you'll be back with Chad."

His words hurt her. They shouldn't have, but they did.

After a heavy silence, Lionel was the first to start talking. Gwen could only listen. Thankfully, he avoided any topics to do with home, and she didn't say anything to change that.

Instead, she tried to convince herself that thirty-two hours of driving was really a long time, and when those hours had passed, she would be grateful to be separated.

"Here we are. This terminal is a lot bigger than the one in Evansville, isn't it?"

"Yes."

She followed him inside, dragging her feet every step of the way.

The dispatcher was a huge, balding man with an enormous potbelly and a cigarette hanging out of his mouth, which Gwen thought was no longer allowed in most workplaces.

"Your load's been delayed," he mumbled around the cigarette. "Won't be ready till late, likely after ten at night."

Gwen turned to Lionel. "It's barely past noon. What are we going to do?"

He shrugged his shoulders. "Nothing we can do. We've got to find some way to kill time."

Gwen checked her watch, but it hadn't changed. "What are we going to do for over ten hours?"

He shrugged his shoulders again. "Usually I either nap or sit around and read. Sometimes I take in a show. Do some grocery shopping. Laundry. Stuff like that."

All those things made sense, but she couldn't see killing ten hours that way. "We don't need to go grocery shopping for days."

His little grin quickened her heart. "I should have guessed you'd think of food first."

Rather than respond in front of the dispatcher, she walked outside, and Lionel followed close behind, snickering all the way. "I have an idea. Women usually like shopping, and we both like eating. Let's combine the two activities. Since both of us only brought jeans and T-shirts, we can go buy ourselves some nice clothes and go somewhere nice for supper, since this is the last of our leisure time. From here, it's straight home. Let's make it a special night together."

Gwen's heart skipped a beat. She'd been thinking so much about this being near the end of their time together, it was almost obsessive. To hear that he also had been contemplating the same thing was strange. She wished she knew how he felt about the matter but was too afraid to know the answer. She swallowed hard. "I'd like that."

She waited while he went back inside to ask the dispatcher for directions. They ended up at a nearby mall where they could park the truck without its being in anyone's way. After enjoying the Funks' hospitality and Freda's good cooking, thinking of the greasy truck stop food over the next couple of days heightened Gwen's anticipation for a fine restaurant meal tonight.

"I've never been shopping for clothes with a woman before. I hope you don't take forever to decide on something and then try on everything in the store three times."

Gwen laughed. "Don't worry. I'm not especially fond of shopping for clothes, so I make my choices quickly. I think part of that comes from shopping with my brother. I can help you pick something nice, too."

"Great. A woman picking my clothes. Isn't this every man's worst nightmare?"

"Depends on your perspective, I guess. Garrett appreciated me picking his clothes. I think part of the reason he likes his job so much is because they provide a uniform, so there's nothing for him to buy except his boots."

It didn't take long to pick a nice shirt and matching slacks for Lionel. She couldn't put her finger on why, but the whole procedure of picking clothes for him was different from picking clothes for her brother. She decided it was because Lionel actually fit the off-the-rack clothes.

For herself, Gwen selected a functional mix-and-match skirt and top that wouldn't crease too badly when she stuffed the outfit into the bottom of her duffel bag. Lionel waited behind her as she waited for a clerk to open the fitting room.

"Going to model it for me?"

"Model it?" she stammered. "Why?"

"Isn't this the time a man is supposed to tell a woman how beautiful she looks when she buys something new?"

She didn't want him to tell her anything of the sort. She didn't want to get too familiar with him as a man. As it was, she had enjoyed holding clothes up to each other and the resulting playful banter far too much. "No, I'm not going to model it. Go sit down somewhere."

After she paid for her purchase, Lionel insisted on carrying both bags. "That wasn't too painful," he said, holding the bags up as if they were some kind of conquest. "And we still have lots of time left before supper."

"We're not done. We have to buy shoes."

"Shoes?"

"I only brought my old beat-up sneakers. Did you bring anything else to wear on your feet?"

"Yes. I always have a pair of black rubber boots in the truck."

She didn't want to give him the dignity of a response. "Let's go in here, they have a sale."

It took them longer to select shoes than the clothing, but finally they managed to choose something relatively inexpensive yet comfortable.

Again, Lionel insisted on carrying all the bags. "I didn't realize buying clothes would be such a major undertaking. And after all this, I keep thinking I'm supposed to buy you jewelry or something."

"I don't wear jewelry. I only wear a watch and earrings. You're safe."

Without warning, his hand wrapped around hers and he stopped dead in his tracks, forcing Gwen to stop as well. She turned to him to see if something was wrong when he stepped closer, leaving only a few inches between them. His voice dropped to a low, gravelly rumble. "Maybe I don't want to be safe."

Her heart pounded. Such strange things had happened to her heart in the past few hours, she wondered if she should see a doctor.

He pointed to a bench a few feet away. "Wait here."

Lionel strode into a jewelry store before she had a chance to protest.

Rather than stand in front of the store with her mouth hanging open, she demurely sat on the bench, looking anywhere other than the jewelry store. He returned in a few minutes, empty-handed. "Let's go back to the truck to change."

Gwen nodded, grateful he hadn't bought anything, and they walked back to the truck. "How are we going to do this?"

"Flip a coin to see who goes first?"

Gwen won the flip, so she told Lionel to change first because she didn't want to wait outside alone all dressed up.

Lionel took only a few minutes, but those few minutes transformed him. Compared to the usual T-shirt and jeans, he was a different man in a long-sleeved cotton shirt and pleated slacks. She tried to imagine what he would look like with the finishing touch of adding a tie, but he didn't need one. He'd changed from attractively rugged to dashingly handsome. Apparently clothes did make the man. He'd even touched up the gel in his hair.

He ran his hand along his jaw. "I wish I could have shaved. And I need a haircut. But this is as good as it gets away from home. Your turn."

Gwen hopped inside and pulled the curtain closed. She'd only remembered at the last minute to buy pantyhose and a slip, and considered it quite unfair that women had to dress in so many layers. She drew the line at buying a new purse when she already had another good purse at home. To make it worse, she hadn't brought any makeup, nor had she brought a curling iron. Even if she would have had the time to use the curling iron or apply the makeup, she refused to buy anything more for one dinner date, especially when this really wasn't a date. It was only Lionel. Her temporary driving partner. And they were only doing something different than the usual routine for dinner. Nothing more.

Getting dressed in the back of the truck was nothing like any other time she'd prepared herself to go out to dinner with a man. The only mirror inside the truck was the rearview mirror, so she didn't get a full look at herself when she was ready. But she didn't need to look. Without makeup and not being able to touch up her hair, she felt plain.

When she emerged from the truck, Lionel held out one hand to help her down.

His smile made her foolish heart flutter. "You look lovely, Gwen."

She didn't think so but didn't want to be impolite and contradict him. Instead, she concentrated on how good Lionel looked. She grinned. "You don't look too bad yourself."

He reached into his pocket. "There's only one thing missing."

"You're not missing anything. You look great."

"Not me. You." He reached into his pants pocket and gave her a small box.

She stared at the small blue velvet box. It was from the jewelry store. "I can't accept this."

He stepped closer and twined the fingers of one hand in her hair. His emerald green eyes bored into her, and his familiar touch seared her to her soul. She had to remind herself that it was only Lionel. "My poor heart will break in two if you turn me down."

She thought he was laying it on a bit thick, but opened the box anyway.

It was a pair of gold earrings, made of a gemstone the same color as the blue of her skirt. She suspected it was a sapphire, surrounded by ribbons of gold dangling down. They were gorgeous. And it didn't take a rocket scientist to know they were also expensive.

"Thank you," she choked out. No man had ever given her a

gift like this before. She'd never had a serious enough relationship with a man where such a gift would have been appro-
priate. "I don't know what to say."

His fingers brushed her cheek. "You've already said thank
you. That's enough." And then his lips brushed hers.

She tried not to enjoy it, but before she had a chance to
think about it, he backed up, and it was over. "Going to put
them on?"

Rather than climb back up into the truck with him standing
behind her, Gwen stepped up on her tiptoes and used the side
mirrors on the truck to change earrings. The simple task had
never been more difficult because she couldn't stop her hands
from shaking. Finally, after a number of failed attempts,
Lionel removed the earrings from her trembling fingers and
slid the earrings in for her.

Very gently he brushed the earrings with his knuckles, then
rested his fingers under her chin. All she could do was stare
into his gorgeous green eyes. If he tried again to kiss her, he
wouldn't have to bend down at all. With the shoes on instead
of her sneakers, they were exactly the same height.

Her eyes drifted shut, but instead of the kiss she expected,
his thumb caressed her lips, then he stepped away.

"They look good on you. Now let's eat. All that shopping
made me hungry."

She didn't resist when he grasped her hand and they began
walking. "It's a block north and two blocks east. We drove by
it on the way to the mall. Looks like a nice place."

"I guess," she mumbled.

The restaurant turned out to be a cozy little place. The
lights were turned down, slow, relaxing strains of music
drifted through the air, and the room was quiet with the total
absence of children.

The hostess showed them to a small booth table in the corner, where Lionel slid in beside her. She was about to tell him
to move and sit across the table from her, but he gave her that

adorable impish grin that made her brain freeze every time. All thoughts of protest fled her mind.

She grabbed the menu and studied it intently. Instead of looking at his own menu, he slid one arm behind her back, snuggled up beside her, then pointed to one of the items listed on her menu. "That's what the dispatcher recommended. He also said the chocolate cheesecake here is excellent, so save room for dessert."

Gwen couldn't concentrate. She could feel his breath on her neck. Not that she didn't expect him to breathe, but it was distracting having him so close. If she turned her head, they'd bump noses.

She snapped the menu closed. "That's what I'll have, then." She didn't know what it was, but she wasn't going to open the menu again.

Without warning, he covered her hand on top of the closed menu.

"I enjoyed going shopping together. It would be nice to do it again some day."

"I don't really like shopping," she mumbled. "What we did today was buy exactly what we went for, then leave. That's the way I always shop."

"I know. I shop that way, too. That's why I like shopping with you."

Gwen shuffled away a couple of inches on the seat and turned to face him, needing to crane her neck back so she could focus on his face, he was so close. All he did was give her a goofy grin. Gwen wondered if maybe he needed glasses or something.

While the waitress took their orders, she slid a respectable distance away.

He opened his mouth to start talking, but Gwen was too nervous about what he would say, so she beat him to it by saying the first thing that popped into her mind. "I used your computer and checked my E-mail earlier. I got a message from my brother Garrett and he was being really strange. He said Robbie's ultrasound was a real eye-opener, which I thought was an odd comment. But I guess that means everything was okay. I couldn't put my finger on exactly what he was getting at. He's probably just overly concerned that she's been so sick."

Gwen snapped her mouth shut, unable to believe what she'd just said. Of all the strange things she'd discussed with Lionel, this time she'd really put her foot in her mouth. A woman didn't discuss morning sickness with a man. With Lionel, once she got started, she couldn't seem to stop herself. He was too easy to confide in.

He leaned back and crossed his arms over his chest, and that dopey grin came back. "Have you ever wondered what it would be like to be as in love as your brother and your friend?"

Gwen sighed and stared into the yellow candle in the center of the table. "What they have is really special. And it's funny. We were all camping together when they fell in love. It hit him right smack between the eyes. I'd never believed in love at first sight until it hit my brother. Everyone saw the signs but him and Robbie. It was almost laughable. He was falling all over himself, behaving like a lovelorn puppy, anything to be close to her. And she couldn't see it. And he didn't know he was acting like an idiot."

Lionel shifted closer, the dopey grin unchanged. "Really?"

"Yes, and they're so different. He lives for the great outdoors, and she'd never done anything outside the city limits. Like night and day, those two. Yet they're perfect for each other."

He flipped a lock of her hair and rested his finger under her chin, leaving her no choice but to meet his gaze. "Does that make you think of anyone else?"

"Yeah. . .Kinda. . ." Gwen stared into his eyes. Lionel was such a handsome man. He was intelligent, but probably very few people realized his potential because he didn't spend long enough in one place for anyone to really know him. She wondered if he knew his neighbors. Uncle Chad's neighbors really didn't know him because he wasn't around in the evenings or on weekends. Being a fellow trucker, Lionel's lifestyle would be the same. She already knew he'd been to what he called his home church only a handful of times because he was out on the road almost every weekend.

At first she had him pegged as the strong, silent type. In a crowd he was thoughtful and serious, but the more she got to know him, the more friendly he became, and he really was a lot of fun once he let his guard down and was away from people. He had a quick wit and an easy laugh, and she had never enjoyed being in anyone's company so much.

Gwen wrapped her hands around her coffee cup and picked it up. "Yes. My friend Molly and her husband Ken are like that, too."

Dinner turned out to be a seafood and steak combination, which Gwen thoroughly enjoyed. Tonight Lionel didn't tease her about the volume she ate. In fact, he didn't tease her about anything. She would never have pegged Lionel for the sensitive male type, but tonight he was different, and she couldn't figure him out.

They lingered a sufficient amount of time after dessert and then left the restaurant.

It was already dark outside, and although the air was still hot, it wasn't uncomfortable. They turned in the direction of the mall, and Gwen held out her hand, expecting him to take it. They'd walked hand in hand on the way to the restaurant.

He picked up her hand, but instead of letting their joined hands dangle between them, he lifted her hand to his mouth. Her knees turned to rubber when he kissed it, let go, and slipped his arm around her waist.

She barely realized they had started to walk. She slipped her arm around his waist for lack of someplace better to put it.

"What are you doing?"

"I'm trying to be romantic. Is it that hard to tell? If it is, then I must be doing something wrong."

Gwen tried not to choke. He wasn't doing anything wrong. But this was Lionel. The man she argued with every day about whose turn it was to crawl under the trailer and check the slack adjusters. She didn't want to be romantic. Yet they were walking down the street arm in arm.

Since they were exactly the same height with her shoes on, every step was in perfect unison, as accurate as marching, except their pace was leisurely and slow. His arm around her waist felt comforting and secure, and right.

They stood outside the truck door while Lionel fished in his pocket for the keys. "I guess this is it. Our date is over."

Date? Gwen swallowed hard. Without question, tonight something had changed between them. She just wasn't sure what. They hadn't merely gone out to share a meal. They had breakfast, lunch, and supper together every day, and nothing about tonight had been the same as any other day. He'd been sweet and kind and attentive to her every need. And he'd been serious in everything he'd said and done.

And he'd kissed her hand. He wasn't trying to comfort her over something she was upset about, nor had panic and mayhem driven them into each other's arms.

There wasn't any other way to describe it. This had really been a date.

He inserted the key into the lock but didn't turn it.

"I want you to know that I will never take advantage of you and never put any pressure on you when we're in the truck. Just like that curtain is the separator for personal privacy, once we get inside the door of that truck, that's the line. We can't do anything that could jeopardize our working relationship in any way, not when we have to stay side by side for days without being able to get away from each other. I like you a lot, Gwen, and the only way I'm going to be able to handle this is to make the rules very specific. I don't know about you, but I can't mix business with pleasure."

Gwen nodded. "No, we can't do that." This wasn't a nine-to-five job; what little space they could call home was mobile. They'd seen each other at their worst; they had no normal routine. There were no boundaries, no rules, no guidelines.

He stepped close to her. "So this is the end of our evening out, where a man takes a woman home. Here we are, our traveling home." His hands cupped her face. "And this is where I kiss you good night."

Gwen's eyes drifted shut, and Lionel kissed her with such an aching sweetness that she didn't want it to end. She wrapped her arms around him and kissed him back, not caring that they were standing in the dark mall parking lot. He was tender and gentle yet held her so firmly that the bond between them was almost a tangible thing. When she thought he was pulling away, he instead tilted his head and kissed her again.

By the time he stopped kissing her, her knees felt wobbly. All she could do was watch as his eyes drifted open very slowly. Very gently he touched her cheek, and then his hand fell to his side, completing the separation.

"Wow," he murmured.

She didn't know what had happened, but she couldn't have expressed it better. Her world would never be the same again. "Yeah," she mumbled back. "Wow."

One corner of his mouth tilted up in a lazy half smile. "Will you still respect me in the morning?"

Gwen blinked. By morning they would be on their way home. In fact, within an hour they were supposed to be on their way home. She shook her head to bring herself back to reality. "Not if we're so late picking up our load that we get fired. You wait out here, I'm going to get changed first."

She yanked the door open and hopped up. Lionel closed it gently behind her once she was inside.

Gwen's hands shook as she pulled her duffel bag out of the bin. Every other time she'd kissed a date good-bye, that was it, it would be days before she saw him again. When a man looked like he was starting to get serious, she always had sufficient time to evaluate the relationship before she saw him again. This time she didn't have that option. Lionel was waiting outside. She wouldn't have that separation for thirty-two hours.

The importance of being so specific about drawing the line between work and their personal lives finally sank into her addled brain. When they were inside the truck and working, there was no room for romance, and that's exactly what was happening. Strange as the situation was, she'd never had such a romantic evening in her life as what she'd just experienced with Lionel, and no man's kiss had ever affected her like this.

Gwen had never changed her clothes so fast in her life. If she couldn't have the time to recover from the rapid change in whatever it was that composed their relationship, and if she couldn't change the setting of being confined inside the truck with him, then the change in clothes was the best she could do to emphasize the separation between a date and work.

She pulled out her grubbiest jeans and oldest T-shirt and slipped her feet into her beat-up old sneakers. As a finishing touch, she messed up her hair.

The transformation was complete.

She was back at work.

twelve

"What do you mean, there's been a change in our running orders?"

The dispatcher tossed the trip envelope through the window onto the counter. "I said the customer got a rush order and put the load for Vancouver off till another day. Now they've got a priority load for Phoenix. They need it picked up as soon as they're finished with it. A doubles team can get it to Phoenix in thirteen hours. And that's you."

Lionel ran his hand down his face. It had taken awhile, but he'd finally managed to focus his thoughts on something else after he'd kissed Gwen and gotten his mind back to where it should have been in the first place: driving.

He'd planned to treat her special and show her how much she meant to him on their last bit of personal time together, but now things had changed. Once they delivered the load in Phoenix, they'd probably have another layover, and he didn't know if he could handle the pressure. He'd crossed the line, and he could never go back. He'd almost told Gwen how much he loved her but had stopped himself before he blurted it out.

If they drove straight through to home, he wouldn't have to worry about crossing the line again, and more than that, if he could keep things professional in the confines of the truck, he wouldn't have to risk hearing that she didn't feel the same way about him. If she didn't, their time together would be unbearable. He couldn't handle that. If she was going to tell him she didn't at least like him a little, he didn't want to hear it until they parted ways, possibly for the last time.

His gut clenched. He didn't want to plan what it would be

like saying good-bye for the last time. He needed more time, but not like this.

"So, what's it gonna be?"

Lionel shook his head to clear his mind. He turned to Gwen. "Have you got a Green Card?"

If she didn't, it was his only chance of refusing the load and getting another load through to Vancouver, and home. Without a Green Card, crossing the border to take their first load to Evansville, they would have to be dispatched straight back home without doing jobs with an American origin and destination. Legally, they got away with delivering the shingles only because it was a mission of mercy after the tornado.

She stiffened. "Of course I've got a Green Card. Uncle Chad made sure of that so we wouldn't get caught in a spot."

So much for that.

By the time they arrived at the client's warehouse, the last pallet was being loaded onto the trailer. They hooked up and were ready to roll before midnight.

"I guess this is what being a doubles team is all about," Gwen said. "The rush loads and unusual stuff."

Lionel was used to rush loads. Every driver got a few rush loads. It was just that the doubles teams got the rush loads that went farther. For him the unusual part was driving with someone else, and then falling in love with the other driver.

He turned to Gwen. "Who sleeps first? You've been driving all night until now, so maybe you'd like a change of pace. If you want to go have a sleep, go ahead."

"That's really nice of you. I think I will. It was hard switching back to regular living hours at the Funks' house, and it's caught up with me. Good night, Lionel."

"Good night, Gwen."

At the sound of the curtain sealing shut, he allowed himself to relax. He'd almost said, "Good night, darling."

He had it bad. The night was going to be a long and lonely one.

ॐ

The sun had been up for hours before Lionel heard the rasp of the Velcro behind him. He smiled and quickly glanced behind him. "Good morning, stranger."

She mumbled something he didn't quite understand.

"Have a good sleep?"

She mumbled something else under her breath.

"What's wrong? Are we not a morning person today?"

This time he thought he understood what she mumbled, and it sounded amazingly similar to "Oh, shut up." Lionel pretended to gasp in shock and caught the dirty look she shot him as she sank into the seat.

Part of him told him not to push his luck, but part of him couldn't leave it alone. "I think you're going to need extra sugar in your coffee this morning. Or is this the kind of morning grumpies that can only be fixed with a double order of fries?"

"It's breakfast time," she grumbled to the window.

"Ah, yes. Time for whole wheat cereal with two percent milk and a glass of orange juice."

This time she didn't answer, and Lionel stayed silent. He wondered what she was really like in the morning, under normal circumstances. So far this was the only day she hadn't been cheerful when she woke up, although he had to remind himself that for two days she'd slept at the Funks' house while he'd slept in the church parking lot.

It struck him that he knew what she liked for breakfast. He wondered how many husbands knew what their wives liked for breakfast.

He stopped at the first place they came to, which happened to be a truck stop. While Gwen freshened up, Lionel headed into the restaurant.

ॐ

Gwen sank quietly into the chair across the table from Lionel. "I'm sorry. I didn't mean to be so crabby. I'm not usually like that in the morning."

"No problem."

There was a problem, but she didn't want to tell him what it was, because he was the problem. For the first time since she'd been out on the road she had not slept well, and it was all his fault.

After their date she had changed clothes in the truck, but he had waited and changed from his nice new clothes to his old jeans and typical T-shirt when they got back to the terminal. The change had hit her in a completely unexpected way. She'd taken one look at him when they got back into the truck, and the first thought that had run through her mind was that the scruffy Lionel was the familiar Lionel, the man she knew, the man she loved.

She was in love with a truck driver.

She noticed he had ordered coffee for her, but he was drinking juice. It felt good to know that at least some of her good habits were rubbing off on him.

He pushed a menu across the table. "This is a switch. For you it's really breakfast time at seven in the morning, but I feel like a bedtime snack. I'm really tired after driving all night. Soon as we eat and get moving, I'm going to crawl into the bunk for a sleep. I hope you don't mind."

"Of course I don't mind." She needed the time to think, but rather than being glad to be rid of him, she felt comforted knowing he was close by, behind the curtain, because she would be thinking about him.

Once the summer was over she wouldn't see him often, if at all. His job as a trucker kept him away from home, and her job as a teacher kept her restricted to staying in town. The only free time she had was on the weekends, and a trucker's busiest times away from home were from Friday to Monday.

It had taken half the night, but she had come to a few conclusions. The first was that for the short time they had left, she wanted to be near him and to spend as much time as she could with him. The professional boundaries, which he had stated were in effect while they were driving together, were perfect and clear. Despite the constant close proximity, there was no temptation, because both of them knew not to cross the line. Personal interaction beyond conversation while driving was unacceptable inside the truck. Inside the truck they were partners only: professional drivers. Anything else would mean disaster, both professionally and personally.

As the meal progressed, she could see he was fading fast, which wasn't surprising. He was long overdue for a sleep, and she felt guilty for sleeping so long. She could see why trucks traveled in convoys and chattered on the CBs. It was necessary to keep each other awake and alert.

He crawled straight into the bunk, and she was sure he was asleep by the time she reached highway speed. The countdown to home had begun, and this stopover in Phoenix gave her extra time to think. This delay was in her favor, and she thanked God for it.

⋙

"I did a good job backing it in, don't you think?" Gwen couldn't help but be proud of herself. It was only her second time backing a load in, and it was straight.

He grinned and winked. "It's okay."

It was better than okay. She'd done a marvelous job. Of course, the lighting helped. The modern facilities were well lit, the compound was paved, and she had lots of room to back in straight.

Gwen yawned, making no effort to hide it. "What now?"

Lionel walked into the customers' building and returned in a few minutes. "I just called dispatch. They don't have a load out for us right away, so we're to call in the morning."

"It is morning. One in the morning."

"Nice try. I saw a motel on the way in with lots of room to park the truck. We'll unhook and go there."

She let Lionel drive while she sagged into the seat. The short time it took to back up into the shipping bay had been more stressful than the entire trip.

Lionel reserved the room while Gwen dug her personal effects out of the bins. Lionel stuck his head through the door. "You've got room twenty-four." He picked up her duffel bag and opened the room for her.

"Wait!" she called. "Can I borrow your computer? I want to check my E-mail. Garrett might have answered me back."

He dumped her stuff on the bed and peeked into the bathroom while she booted up the computer.

"This is great." His voice echoed as he spoke into the bathroom. "Don't turn in the key in the morning, I want to have a real shower. And I'll wait for you to be finished with my computer. I've got some stuff to catch up on while you sleep."

Gwen phoned the clerk for an outside line and set the modem to dial while Lionel opened all the drawers in the small desk.

"Hey! A Gideon Bible! Cool!" He turned, grinned, and started flipping through it. "I check for these every time I need to rent a room."

Gwen mumbled her approval while a long E-mail came through. "You'd better read this. It's from Uncle Chad."

He read the message over her shoulder.

Hi, Gwen,
   Hope you're having a great time on the road with Lionel. Like I said before, he's a good Christian and a righteous man and I know he'll treat you right.

Lionel puffed out his chest. "See? A good reference from your uncle. I see the beginning of a beautiful relationship."

Gwen smacked him in the arm. "Quit fooling around. This is important. Keep reading."

The truck is fixed, right on time, and until you return, they have me running singles. As an unofficial favor, the dispatchers have put me on low priority runs in order to give me more time at home, including weekends.

I know I can't ask you to stay away forever, but if things are working out with you and Lionel, it would give me a very special time with the family if you could stay out on the road a while longer. At the time I am writing this, you are somewhere between Topeka and Phoenix. The longer you are gone, the more time I have with my family. This is a rare opportunity for us, but I don't want to put you in an uncomfortable position with Lionel. This is being done as a favor only and cannot go on indefinitely. But they will pass the word amongst the dispatchers not to send you and Lionel home to Vancouver for a little while longer if you agree. Whatever you decide, I will understand.

Love always,
Uncle Chad

"Wow," Lionel muttered. "What are you going to do?"

Gwen looked up at him as he stood beside her. "I don't know. What do you think?"

The silence dragged. Lionel turned to stare at the bed in the middle of the motel room and rammed his hands into his pockets. "We should pray and talk about it in the morning."

Gwen's heart nearly stopped. They'd prayed together many times, and every time they had, they had sat together and joined hands. But that was never in the middle of a motel room.

He picked up his laptop. "I'll see you in the morning. Good night." He walked out in the blink of an eye, without turning around.

Gwen closed the door and watched him through the crack of the curtain as he hopped up inside the truck. The light went on in the bunk area as he set up the table to get ready to do his paperwork on the computer.

She had assumed he meant they should pray together, but he'd obviously meant in private. She wanted to pray with him. It would have been right to pray together. But not proper to do so sitting on the bed in a motel.

Gwen changed into her pajamas and crawled into bed, preparing herself to talk to God about the decision she had to make.

Of course, Uncle Chad wanted to take advantage of this limited opportunity to spend more time at home. Whenever he booked off, he didn't get paid, and under his contract he couldn't book time off unless it was for specified vacation time or something critical.

Over the years she had seen many times where her aunt had nearly broken down, she'd missed her husband so much. As an adult, Gwen could understand the anguish of separation of a husband and wife, different from the way her cousins missed their father.

She wanted him to spend more time with Aunt Chelsea and her cousins. But at what cost to her?

Gwen stared blankly at the closed curtains, knowing that on the other side was Lionel in his truck.

If she decided to go straight home, she would be denying Uncle Chad something she knew had been difficult for him to ask. Would she be selfish to refuse?

If she decided to continue driving with Lionel, what would happen? She enjoyed being with him, both when they were driving, or not. Except for his being a loner and a truck driver, she couldn't help but love him. But what would happen if she stayed with him?

She was an adult and a Christian, but that didn't mean she was immune to temptation. She would be setting herself up for torture if she continued driving with him and had to maintain an emotional distance. Could she handle the situation if she said yes? Could she live with herself if she said no?

Gwen closed her eyes and prayed like she'd never prayed before.

≈

Lionel stared up at the ceiling of the truck. He'd given up on his paperwork. He'd been lying in the dark for hours, but he still couldn't sleep.

They'd just been given the perfect excuse not to go home, to spend days, even weeks, exclusively with each other.

Not that doing Chad a favor wasn't a good thing, but he wanted her to do it because she wanted to be with him, not just for Chad's sake. However, the impropriety of the situation they found themselves in was even more of a stumbling block now. Until now, traveling together had been beyond their control, something thrust upon them when there was nothing either of them could do about it. Now it had become a choice.

They needed to pray about this together, but he wasn't going to hold hands and sit on a bed in a motel room to do so. He loved Gwen with all his heart and soul. He wanted to spend the rest of his life with her, to make her his wife and the mother of his children. God said to flee from temptation, and even though it meant not praying together, he'd flown. He needed to outline the hands-off rules in the truck for a reason, and those rules applied tenfold in a motel room.

Lionel rolled onto his stomach and buried his face in the pillow. He knew what he wanted, but what did Gwen want?

Above all, did she trust him?

Did he trust himself?

The matter was out of his hands. It was Gwen's decision for now, but ultimately it was God's direction that would determine what would happen tomorrow and in the days and weeks to follow. He knew what he wanted but didn't know what was best, or right. Rather than pray for his own selfish desires, he rolled over, once again on his back, pressed his hands over his heart, squeezed his eyes shut, and spoke out loud, "Father God, Thy will be done!"

Peace filled his soul. The future was out of his hands, and in God's, where it belonged.

Lionel rolled over and managed to drift off to sleep until his ringing cell phone jolted him out of his dreams.

After listening to the dispatcher, he threw on his clothes, hurried outside, and knocked on Gwen's door. He shouldn't have been surprised to see her already dressed and ready to go. After all, it was daylight.

"The dispatcher just called. We've got to go now. Give me a few minutes to shower."

She waited for him in the truck, and when he was done, they drove the three blocks to the terminal in silence. He usually teased her to see if she'd slept well. This time he wasn't in the mood to joke around. Not a word was said when they walked together into the dispatch office.

The day shift dispatcher held two envelopes in his hands. "You've got a choice between two loads: a through load for Vancouver, or a consolidation, then a couple of drop shipments ending up in Buffalo. Both are ready now. What'll it be?"

Lionel clenched his teeth so hard his jaw hurt. The dispatcher stared at him, expecting it to be Lionel to make the decision. Lionel kept silent and looked at Gwen. His heart was pounding and his palms were sweating. He forced himself to breathe. Gwen turned to him. All he could do was nod once.

The dispatcher turned to Gwen.

Gwen stiffened her back, sucked in a deep breath, and turned to face the dispatcher.

The seconds ticked on like hours.

Lionel thought he might throw up.

thirteen

Gwen swallowed past the frog in her throat. "Buffalo," she said.

The dispatcher handed her the envelope from his right hand, but her hands were shaking too much to open it, so she turned and held it out to Lionel.

His face was pale, his eyes were wide open, and he didn't move, not even to raise his hand to take the envelope from her as she held it in front of him.

His voice came out in a hoarse croak. "Buffalo? Are you serious?"

"Yes." She still could barely believe her own answer. She would be lying if she said she was doing it as a favor to Uncle Chad. The favor was merely a good excuse. She was going to Buffalo because she wanted to spend more time with Lionel.

Last night she'd prayed for God to tell her to go home. No such answer came.

The boundaries and codes of conduct were stated before their feelings for each other became an issue. He made her feel safe, and she trusted him. It had stung for only a minute when he bolted out of the motel room. More than anything, she saw the actions of a man who didn't cross any lines best left alone.

God's rules and boundaries gave freedom instead of restrictions. If she followed the guidelines of God's Word for her life, she had the complete freedom, providing she made wise and moral choices, to follow the desires of her heart. As soon as they returned home, whatever was between them would be over. God had provided a way to make it last a little longer, and for that she was grateful.

She felt the envelope pulling out of her fingers. Lionel

cupped her elbow and ushered her outside. "I think we have to talk. In private."

They walked outside but didn't go to the truck. It seemed like neither of them wanted it to be that private.

"You're sure about this?"

All she could do was nod.

The color returned to his face, and he smiled. "Then let's see what we've got." He opened the flap and pulled out a stack of papers, mumbling as he read the top sheet. "We leave here and go to El Paso and pick up a part load, then we start a series of drop shipments. All the bills of lading are here. Directions, too." He paged through them one at a time, still muttering under his breath. "San Antonio, Oklahoma City, Birmingham, then the final drop in Buffalo." He slapped the heel of his palm to his forehead, still holding the wad of papers, and squeezed his eyes shut. "This is the most screwball series of drop shipments I've ever seen! These are all short hops in between; we'll be spending all our time in layovers!"

"Should we go back and take the Vancouver load?"

His face paled instantly. "No!" A blush spread over his cheeks, and his ears turned red. He cleared his throat, and his voice lowered in volume. "I mean, this is just fine. It's just the kind of thing you would love as a beginning driver. This is what's known as a paid tourist run. We can take our time, and you can probably even get some good pictures. Providing we're somewhere it's worth taking pictures."

Gwen beamed. "Great! I was beginning to wonder if I would get a chance to use my camera."

Lionel's voice changed to a melodic intonation. "Then we shuff-le off to Buff-a-lo." He grinned and stuffed all the papers back in the envelope.

"If you start singing, I'm going back and taking the Vancouver load."

He laughed and darted toward the truck before she could snatch the envelope out of his hand. "Catch me if you can!" he called out as he ran.

Gwen smiled and walked to the truck. She had done the right thing.

***

"I think you're wrong. I don't understand why you say this is going to be a wacky trip." She'd entered the dates and the destinations in the computer three times, and every time the answers were the same.

"It's because that program doesn't allow for the most important variable."

"I thought you said this program was the best."

"It doesn't account for fickle clients."

"Oh."

Gwen figured out that if all went well, since today was Thursday, they could be at the final destination Saturday, which she figured wasn't bad at all. Lionel had just laughed and reminded her that the customers didn't keep the same hours they did.

So far all had gone well. They'd arrived in El Paso at six in the evening on Wednesday. It had taken an hour for the customer to finish loading. They'd eaten another wonderful truck stop meal and left at eight. It was now Thursday just after sunrise. They were going to pull into San Antonio, the first point where they'd have to unload something, and then they would keep going.

"Let's go to the customer's warehouse first. We can eat and shower after we unload, which should take us to lunch time."

"Sure." Gwen packed up the computer. She was becoming accustomed to using Lionel's laptop while they were moving. Using her big desktop computer at the school would never be the same.

"Who gets to back it in?"

Gwen stuck her tongue out at him. "I'm a passenger. You do it."

Everything went smoothly, and soon they were at the truck stop outside of town. After they finished fueling and showered, Gwen took the laptop into the truck stop and downloaded their

E-mail, then took the laptop into the restaurant.

Lionel sipped his coffee while she opened the Inbox.

"You're like a kid with a new toy with that thing," he grumbled. "Will you give it a rest?"

"I told you, I'm expecting something from my brother. There's nothing for me, but you got something from your friend Randy. The subject title is 'Happy Birthday.' Is it your birthday?"

He took another long sip. "Whatever."

"It is! Why didn't you tell me? How old are you?"

"It's not a big deal. I'm thirty-two."

"Well, happy thirty-second birthday. I could have at least gotten you a card."

"I don't want a card. It's just clutter in the truck."

"Then I can get you a piece of cake. Give me the dessert menu."

"If you have even the remotest idea of ordering a piece of cake with a candle on it, I'm leaving."

"If you think I'd do that to you, then you don't know me very well."

"Sorry," he mumbled. "Someone did that to me once, and I never want to go through that again for the rest of my life."

Gwen watched him stare into the bottom of his coffee cup. On a number of occasions she'd been the instigator to set up singing waiters, sparklers for candles on a cake, and the whole package for a birthday in a restaurant. However, she would never consider doing that to Lionel. Whoever did that must not have known him very well. "I can't imagine who would do that to you."

"It was my ex-fiancée," he mumbled.

Gwen couldn't stifle a gasp.

"Yes, I was engaged once. A few weeks before what was supposed to be our wedding day, I came home early and found her with someone else."

"Oh. . .Lionel. . .I'm so sorry. . ."

He swished around the dribbles in the bottom of the cup,

not looking up. "Don't be sorry. It hurt at the time, but shortly after that I met Jesus. We wouldn't have been right for each other, I can see that now."

Gwen thought of the few relationships she'd had with men, none of which had ever come close to being serious. "Still, it must have been awful."

"I lived." He checked his watch. "I don't feel like sitting around here. Let's go."

Not a word was said as they walked to the truck, but she didn't like him being so sullen. It wasn't like him. She didn't want to make a big deal of it, if Lionel didn't want a fuss. Still, everyone deserved something special on their birthday. She knew they would be driving straight through to Oklahoma City, so she didn't have time to buy him a small gift or even a card, which she would have done, despite his calling such things clutter.

While he inserted the key in the lock, Gwen laid the laptop on the running board and stepped between Lionel and the truck.

"What are you doing?" he asked.

She cupped his chin in her hands. "Happy birthday, Lionel."

And she kissed him. Not just a little brush-on-the-lips kiss, but a real, big, loud, smacking kiss. She even made a popping sound when she pulled away.

"Hey!"

She snatched up the laptop, pulled the keys out of the lock, opened the door, and hopped in before he had a chance to regain his bearings. "I thought you said we should go. I'm driving."

By the time they pulled into Oklahoma City it was ten at night. The client's warehouse was closed up, but a night watchman opened the gate and told them to back the trailer in and leave it until morning.

Since they had all the time in the world, Gwen backed it in, taking her time and trying it a number of times just for the practice. Together they cranked down the dolly legs and set the trailer brakes.

Gwen peeked under the trailer and called out to Lionel. "If you knew this would happen where we'd be stuck here like this in the middle of the night, we should have stopped in Dallas."

"What for?"

"I've never been to Dallas."

Lionel shook his head. "We're in a truck and pulling a fifty-three-foot trailer. We can't exactly go touring around the city and visiting all the local hot spots."

"I could at least have taken some pictures."

"You got a picture of the skyline."

Gwen rested her hands on her hips. "That was from out the window, and we were moving at the time."

"Well, here we are in Oklahoma City, and we're not going anywhere. Take all the pictures you want."

"It's midnight!"

"There's lots of stars to take pictures of. Look. There's the Big Dipper." He pointed up. "And there's Polaris, which the Big Dipper points to. It's the tail of Ursa Minor, which is supposed to be a bear, but most people call it the Little Dipper."

"That's fascinating. How did you know that?"

"I spend a lot of time in the middle of nowhere in the middle of the night, so I've had time to study the sky. It's really quite remarkable."

Gwen looked up. Not a cloud disturbed the crystal-clear images of the night. The beauty of God's creation shining above had always awed her, but it had never touched her like right now. "It doesn't have the same feel from the industrial estate as it does from a deserted rest area off the highway, does it?"

"Nope."

If it wasn't for the concrete and buildings around them, the setting would have been rather romantic. The quiet night, the beauty of the stars above, and, most of all, the kind and handsome man beside her. The night watchman had gone back to his post at the gate, leaving them alone. It was the perfect time and place for Lionel to kiss her, and not a silly, smacking kiss like she'd given him on his birthday, but a real, sizzling, melt-your-socks-off type of kiss.

"It's late. We've got to get up early in the morning and get going, so I'll drop you off at a motel. I'll drive."

જ

Lionel couldn't believe he was doing this. He'd consented to wait inside the truck while Gwen ran into a large wholesale mega-store for a few groceries. He again checked his watch and questioned her definition of the word *quick*. He'd managed to get some reading done, but he'd been too distracted to really concentrate. He wanted to be with her, and the waiting was killing him.

Once they arrived back home, he didn't know how he was ever going to run singles again. At first he'd worried that being with someone would drive him nuts, but instead he was going nuts without her. She'd been gone less than an hour.

"I'm back. Let's go."

She tossed a small bag into the fridge, and then hoisted a large box behind the seat. A bag around it prevented him from seeing the markings.

"What in the world is that?"

"It's a surprise. I thought you were in a rush to get moving."

He studied the box. For the size of it, apparently it wasn't heavy.

"Mind your own business! Now get going."

He almost made a teasing comment about a nagging wife but stopped himself in time. He wondered what it would be like to be married to Gwen. If he'd been anxious for her return when she was only at the store, what would it be like for the long separations when she was tied to the school and he was out on the road?

They picked up the trailer, turned the music on loud, and headed to Birmingham.

Conversation was light and playful until mid-afternoon, when Gwen was suddenly silent. After a couple of minutes she spoke again. "I've been thinking."

Lionel cringed. "Uh oh."

"If we just drove like normal, we'd arrive Saturday at three-thirty in the morning, and no one is going to be there. I was thinking that we should kill some time out here. Relax, take it easy, and enjoy ourselves away from the city. We really don't have to be there until eight-thirty in the morning, so let's do that."

He had a feeling there was more to her suggestion than met the eye. "What have you got in mind?"

"I want you to stop at the next rest area."

That was easy. Too easy. But he did anyway.

Once in the parking area, he killed the engine and reached for the door handle.

"No! You wait in the truck."

"Gwen. . .You're making me nervous."

"I have a surprise for you."

Now she really was making him nervous.

She pulled the box outside, but before she closed the truck door, she shot him a quelling look.

Lionel laughed. The woman could definitely hold her own, and he loved it. If they did pursue their relationship after their driving together was over, he knew Gwen possessed the strength to endure the separations. However, he wasn't sure he did.

"You can come out now!"

Gwen stood beside the picnic table, the large white bag covering something large in the center.

"Tah-dah!" She whipped off the bag.

"It's a portable barbecue."

She grinned from ear to ear. "Yes!"

"Okay. . ."

"I'm going to barbecue supper today. We've got lots of time."

Visions of baked potatoes and medium-rare T-bone steak danced through his mind. He loved barbecued corn on the cob, steamed to perfection after being wrapped tightly in tinfoil. Or mushrooms would be even better.

"I bought those special foot-long wieners, and whole wheat hot dog buns. And carrots. And I even got a can of beans. I didn't know if you had a can opener, so I bought one, just in case. I love cold beans."

"Uh. . .sounds delicious."

Her grin widened. "This is my favorite camping meal. When I first started talking about driving a truck with Uncle Chad, I compared it to camping. Now that I've been doing it, I can see some things are the same, but not really."

"That makes sense."

"Never mind. Here, you scrape the carrots."

The domesticness of what they were doing hit him in the gut like a sucker punch. Gwen chattered away about camping and the school and her family, but all he could think about was what it would be like if they had a family of their own. About what it would be like to spend quality time together. Kids playing at their feet, and then settling in for some private time together when all was quiet for the night.

The healthful whole wheat buns seemed to contrast the questionable food value of the wieners, but he was surprised to find how much he enjoyed the simple meal. He also admired Gwen's ingenuity at the small disposable propane cartridge she'd purchased rather than the large cylinder on most propane barbecues.

"You've been awful quiet. What's on your mind?"

Marriage. Kids. A house in the country. A dog. Little league games. "Nothing in particular."

When all was tidied up and the small barbecue packed up inside the truck, they lay on their backs on the grass to enjoy the sunset until the stars began to wink their way out in the evening sky. When they started to feel the chill from lying on the grass, they walked back to the truck and headed to Alabama.

❧

Gwen checked her watch. "What's taking them so long? I thought this was supposed to be a priority shipment."

"This is another thing that the computer program doesn't

take into account. Overtime. The people who got called in are on overtime since it's Saturday. One of them told me that if they work for four hours they get paid for the day, at time-and-a-half. So if I count on my fingers correctly, we will be out of here at precisely one in the afternoon."

"That's not right."

"That's the way it goes."

Gwen sighed. She knew that she was sheltered from such things as a teacher, and she knew the course of human nature, but to be delayed by something that she felt was cheating an employer, even if it wasn't her employer, annoyed her. "We don't have any choice, do we?"

"Nope."

By the time they were done, Gwen was more than ready to go. She almost laughed at herself. When she'd first started driving with Lionel, his compulsion to always keep the load moving annoyed her, and now she was no different.

This time Lionel had a nap in the afternoon, and she slept earlier in the evening than usual as they traveled. Both of them were wide awake in the middle of the night, so rather than getting a motel, they kept going. They caught the sunrise just over the New York state line. Since she was driving, Lionel took a picture out the window with her camera.

"I'm going to miss being in church on Sunday," Gwen sighed. "I can't remember the last time I missed a service, I mean, not counting since I started driving with Uncle Chad."

"We don't necessarily have to miss. Lots of the truck stops have small chapels for truckers passing through."

"Really?"

"Really. And I just happen to have a directory of where they are." He pulled a little book out of the glove box. "We're in luck. We're not far away from one right now."

"Really?"

He grinned. "Really."

Gwen pulled into the parking lot of the truck stop as directed, and they walked around the back to a long narrow building that looked suspiciously like a converted trailer. The only windows were in the back doors, and it was so small there was room only for one row of pews down the side, with a small altar at the front. Gwen thought it rather cozy, and not too different from the Funks' little church, except this one was a very miniature makeshift version. She noted Bibles in the pews, as well as tracts everywhere, including on a small table in the back.

At the front, a fiftyish man dressed in a western style shirt and jeans, who was probably the minister, was talking and laughing with another man whom Gwen pegged as another trucker.

"It's so early. What time do things usually start?"

"Usually at seven-thirty. This is all volunteer time for the minister. Services are short. And after they're over, no one hangs around because most of the ministers have their own congregations to go to for regular Sunday services. Besides, we're all wayfaring strangers who have schedules to keep for early Monday and have to keep moving."

"That makes sense, I guess."

A few more men entered while they spoke. Right at seven-thirty the minister stood at the front and welcomed everyone.

Gwen leaned to whisper in Lionel's ear. "There are only eight people here, including us. And I'm the only woman!"

He leaned back to whisper his reply. "I hope you didn't expect any different. The most I've ever seen on Sunday morning is a dozen, and I do this a lot."

She straightened and waited as the minister slipped a tape into the machine and hit the button.

If Lionel was used to such small gatherings, it would explain why he was so stiff at the Funks' church, which she considered small compared to the upwards of four hundred people who attended her church back home.

The music came on, a few good old-time gospel songs, and the small gathering of people sang heartily. Gwen enjoyed hearing the low male voices, as back home the prominent voices she heard were female. It set a different mood to the worship time.

The minister preached an enthusiastic sermon on the miracles of Jesus, and although it was short, it was refreshing after a busy and long week on the road.

". . .and go with God's good wishes!"

Everyone stood. Three of the men immediately went outside and drove away, two of the other drivers stood outside and talked, and the same man who was there when they first arrived began talking to the minister again.

Gwen followed Lionel outside and stood outside the small building where the sun was bright and the summer breeze ruffled her hair. "It's been a long time since I've heard such a good evangelical message."

"Yes. I gave my heart to Jesus at a service very similar to this."

Without saying so, Gwen had a feeling it wasn't long after his ex-fiancée broke his heart. She couldn't imagine what it would be like to go through such heartache.

"Whenever I'm close to Fargo, I always stop in at that little chapel, or else the church run by the pastor who runs it. He's an ex-trucker turned minister, and he really knows what it's like to live like this."

"That's really nice." Gwen smiled and rested her hand on Lionel's arm. "And that was a lovely service."

"I don't know if any of those truckers or the minister would appreciate you calling it *lovely*.

"You know what I meant. So, now what?"

"We shuffle off to Buffalo, get a room for you when we get there, unload at seven A.M., and go to the terminal to see what kind of outbound load they've got for us. Then we're on the road again."

fourteen

Lionel stared at the gray building looming before him. After all these years, it was so familiar, even though it had been a month since he'd last seen it. At this moment he hated it. They were home. It was over.

He couldn't think of anything worthwhile to say, so he said nothing. They walked to the dispatch office in silence together. For the last time.

Burt took their trip sheets and logbooks. "Long time, no see, Lionel. And if it isn't the other half of our doubles team. Now that you're back, Jeff is ready to drive again, so it looks like you came home just to be replaced." Burt laughed at his own comment.

Lionel didn't find Burt the least bit amusing. He noticed Gwen didn't have anything to say, either. Lionel emptied out his over-stuffed mail slot, and they turned and walked out.

He drove Gwen home and helped carry her personal belongings inside. Over the past month she'd accumulated much more than the one duffel bag, sleeping bag, and pillow he'd carried into his truck when he picked her up at the side of the road at Snoqualmie.

She told him to keep the barbecue, to consider it a belated birthday gift. He'd never received such a special gift in his life.

They stood in the open doorway.

Gwen studied the ground and shuffled her feet. "It feels strange to be home."

"I know what you mean. It's the same with me. After being gone a long time, it's familiar, but it's not."

Silence hung in the air.

Gwen shuffled her feet again. "Strange as it sounds, the

first thing I'm going to do is have a long, hot bath. With bubble bath."

He smiled. "Same. Just with no bubbles."

More silence hung between them.

Lionel grasped her hands and cleared his throat. "Can we continue seeing each other? I'd like to call you when I'm in town and take you out and stuff."

"Yes, I'd like that."

"So I guess this is it."

Her sad little smile ripped him in two. If he had to say good-bye to the woman he loved, he was going to do it right. He threw his arms around her and kissed her with everything he had in him until the sound of someone walking by caused them to separate.

He stared into her beautiful brown eyes. Eyes that were starting to well up with tears.

He couldn't watch her cry. Not like this.

"See you sometime," he croaked out.

Before she could reply, he walked to the truck as quickly as his dignity would allow and drove home.

In an attempt to settle himself, he proceeded through what had always been his normal routine after getting back from a long trip. Nothing helped. He sorted through his mail, listened to the messages on his answering machine, and got his laundry started. He didn't want to open the fridge. Even his cactus was dead.

He'd only just dropped her off a few hours ago, but already he felt the gaping void in his life.

He needed her in so many ways. She was attractive in all the ways a man found a woman attractive, but most of all, seeing each other at their best and their worst, in addition to falling in love with her, she'd become his best friend.

They had no future together. She was bound to her job as a teacher, working days and off weekends, and he was limited to the hours of his trips, leaving evenings and away all weekend.

He stared out into the night from his apartment's balcony. The lights of the city glowed beneath him, the headlights of moving cars streaked down the roads in little white lines. Echoes of honking horns and the roar of the odd car reached him even at the twenty-fifth floor. He'd always found peace watching the city from a distance, untouched by the commotion of life below. Tonight it only made him feel lonely.

He slid the patio door closed behind him. In the quiet of his small kitchen, he began the last untouched chore—digging through what had accumulated in the company mail slot in his absence. He found the usual forms questioning his handwriting on a few log entries, fuel bills, and a warranty reminder. At the bottom of the pile, he found a tape.

Lionel picked it up. A Post-it note attached identified it as being from Gwen, put there when she'd just begun her second trip out, the day of Chad's breakdown in Snoqualmie. On her first trip she'd promised him a tape of the sermon they'd talked about over the CB radio. Since she hadn't expected to see him, she'd tucked it in his mail slot for when he got back.

The label identified the topic as "Friendship—God's Way."

He slipped the tape into his cassette player but couldn't press the button to listen to it. Lionel knew it was going to describe someone he'd just left, someone he wanted to share his life with, but by the nature of their lifestyles they would seldom cross paths, until they drifted apart forever.

He didn't listen to the tape. He crawled into bed and stared at the ceiling all night.

❧

Gwen stared at the pile of books on her table for the courses she'd be teaching in the coming school year.

Very gently she touched her earrings. The earrings Lionel had given her in Topeka. She hadn't taken them off since she'd been home.

She studied her class list for the coming year. As their teacher, she had always thought she would make an impact on all the young lives she touched. But now, looking at the names, even knowing that some might, one day, remember her fondly in years to come, in almost all cases she was just another ship that passed in the night. Once they left her classroom, she would never see them again.

Gwen fingered the earrings again. She hadn't seen Lionel for nearly two weeks, the longest two weeks of her life. She'd received many E-mails, loaded with typing errors and apologies for them. Many he signed with his CB handle, The Lion King. They were all bittersweet. She didn't want to read his words; she wanted to hear his voice. In person.

She'd made the biggest mistake of her life when she agreed to keep driving with him. While she'd enjoyed their time together, the love between them had blossomed in a way neither of them could have foreseen. Yet they never talked about it. They were both too aware that it couldn't last. When he'd kissed her good-bye at the door two weeks ago, it was more than saying good-bye to the man she loved. She was also saying good-bye to her best friend. Ripping off her right arm couldn't have hurt any more.

Gwen reached for the phone. She wasn't doing herself any good by dwelling on it. Instead of getting herself even more depressed, Gwen needed to talk to someone, and the person who could best make her laugh was her friend Molly.

At the same second she touched the phone, the doorbell rang.

It was Lionel. He stood in the doorway, holding a single red rose. "I've missed you."

Gwen's throat clogged. She could barely choke the words out. "I've missed you, too."

She didn't ask if he wanted to come in. She didn't need to. Gwen put the rose in a glass of water, and they sat together on the couch.

Lionel grasped both her hands. "There's something I have to tell you. I'm going to sell the truck."

Gwen's stomach knotted. Driving a truck was all he'd ever done. It was his life. If he'd just discovered a fatal medical condition that was forcing him to quit, she didn't know what she would do. She struggled to speak past the tightness in her throat. "Why?"

"These last two weeks have been the worst of my life. I can't do this anymore. Not without you."

She couldn't think of a thing to say. She opened her mouth to tell him that she had been miserable without him, too, but he touched his index finger to her lips. "Please let me finish. I've thought a lot about this; it's not a decision I've made lightly."

Gwen nodded and he lowered his finger.

"I can't leave you for days and weeks at a time. These last two weeks have been. . .well, not good. I couldn't live like that indefinitely."

She opened her mouth to tell him she would never be unfaithful, but he spoke before she could say a word. "You promised you'd let me finish. I know what you're thinking, and you're wrong. You're nothing like Sharon, I know you won't find someone else while I'm gone. I don't want to stop driving because I don't trust you. It's because I miss you too much, and driving just hasn't been satisfying anymore without you."

"I don't know what to say."

His grip on her hands tightened. "I love you, Gwen. Until I find a buyer, I'll still have to drive, but whenever I'm in town, I want to spend all the time we can together. I'll do whatever I can to make this work. And if that means quitting driving, then that's what I'm going to do."

Gwen gulped. "Make this work?"

He shook his head. "I'm doing this all wrong. What I really came here to do was to ask if you'd marry me. And if it's too sudden, then we'll date and stuff until you're as sure as I am that this is God's will for us, to love each other forever, to have and to hold, for better, for worse, for richer, for poorer. The whole package. I love you, Gwen. Will you marry me?"

Gwen's vision blurred. "I love you, too. And yes, I'll marry you. Under one condition. Don't sell the truck."

His kiss was immediate and welcome. When his mouth released hers, he held her firmly in his arms, and she never wanted him to let go.

"I don't care about the truck," he mumbled into her hair.

"Well, I do," she said. "I loved living on the road. But I don't think it's something I could do forever. Like when it's time to have children. About a year driving together sounds good, though."

He murmured her name and buried his face farther in her hair, but otherwise didn't speak.

"I'll take a leave of absence from teaching and drive with you. Uncle Chad says Burt is going to retire in about a year, and he heard Burt mention your name as a possibility for his replacement. Do you think you'd like that?"

He cupped her face in his hands. "Yes, I would. And I'd love to drive with you again. But, before you step foot in that truck again, you need more than your Class-One license. You need a marriage license. And then we'll run doubles again."

Gwen grinned. "Really?"

Lionel nodded. "Really."

"And does that mean I get my name painted on the door? You've got 'The Lion King' painted on the driver's door."

"After we get married, that will make you 'The Lion Queen.' How's that?"

"And that makes the truck 'The Lion's Den.' And then we'll be. . ."

Lionel grinned. ". . .On the road again."

A Letter To Our Readers

Dear Reader:

In order that we might better contribute to your reading enjoyment, we would appreciate your taking a few minutes to respond to the following questions. We welcome your comments and read each form and letter we receive. When completed, please return to the following:

Rebecca Germany, Fiction Editor
Heartsong Presents
PO Box 719
Uhrichsville, Ohio 44683

1. Did you enjoy reading *On the Road Again?*
   ☐ Very much. I would like to see more books
      by this author!
   ☐ Moderately
      I would have enjoyed it more if _____

      _____

      _____

2. Are you a member of **Heartsong Presents**?   Yes ☐   No ☐
   If no, where did you purchase this book? _____

   _____

3. How would you rate, on a scale from 1 (poor) to 5 (superior),
   the cover design? _____

4. On a scale from 1 (poor) to 10 (superior), please rate the
   following elements.

   _____ Heroine   _____ Plot

   _____ Hero   _____ Inspirational theme

   _____ Setting   _____ Secondary characters

5. These characters were special because_____

_____

_____

6. How has this book inspired your life?_____

_____

_____

7. What settings would you like to see covered in future
   Heartsong Presents books?_____

_____

_____

8. What are some inspirational themes you would like to see
   treated in future books?_____

_____

_____

9. Would you be interested in reading other **Heartsong
   Presents** titles?   Yes ❑   No ❑

10. Please check your age range:
    ❑ Under 18   ❑ 18-24   ❑ 25-34
    ❑ 35-45   ❑ 46-55   ❑ Over 55

11. How many hours per week do you read?_____

Name _____

Occupation _____

Address _____

City _____ State _____ Zip _____

Hearts♥ng Presents
Love Stories Are Rated G!

That's for godly, gratifying, and of course, great! If you love a thrilling love story, but don't appreciate the sordidness of some popular paperback romances, **Heartsong Presents** is for you. In fact, **Heartsong Presents** is the *only inspirational romance book club* featuring love stories where Christian faith is the primary ingredient in a marriage relationship.

Sign up today to receive your first set of four, never before published Christian romances. Send no money now; you will receive a bill with the first shipment. You may cancel at any time without obligation, and if you aren't completely satisfied with any selection, you may return the books for an immediate refund!

Imagine. . .four new romances every four weeks—two historical, two contemporary—with men and women like you who long to meet the one God has chosen as the love of their lives. . . all for the low price of $9.97 postpaid.

To join, simply complete the coupon below and mail to the address provided. **Heartsong Presents** romances are rated G for another reason: They'll arrive *Godspeed!*